The Mysterious Mystery Man

The Mysterious Mystery Man

The Adventures of Prince and Ashley, Book 2

Justin T. Miller

This book is a work of fiction. Names, characters, places, and incidents are either the product of the author's imagination or are used fictitiously, and any resemblance to actual persons, living or dead, business establishments, events, or locales is entirely coincidental.

Published by BooRoo Publishing
Walnut Creek, California
Printed in the U.S.A.

Library of Congress Control Number: 2021912866

ISBN: 0-578-94162-7
ISBN 13: 978-0-578-94162-2

First paperback edition, 2021

For my family, my friends, and all the children who read my first book and inspired me to write my second book.

CONTENTS

CHAPTER 1

ARRIVING AT THE AIRPORT

Ashley Julia Pea used to not have many close friends, and her life used to be really boring. Everything seemed to change after she met Prince last year. Prince's full name was Miles Prince Gold, but everyone just called him Prince because of his middle name.

Prince and Ashley became best friends last year, and they had some amazing adventures before the school year ended. But then summer vacation happened, and they were both very sad since they could not see each other for a very long time.

A few months ago, Prince and his dad, Dr. Gold, had to move all the way across the country to Washington, D.C., which is the capital of the

United States. The capital is the place where a lot of the country's leaders live and work. It is also the place where the President of the United States lives with his family. Dr. Gold and Prince were only supposed to be gone for a few weeks, but the President personally asked Dr. Gold to stay the entire summer so he could work on a secret government science project.

It was the last week of summer vacation before school started when Prince was finally coming back home with his dad, Dr. Gold. Their airplane ride from Washington, D.C., left extremely early in the morning, so Prince was very tired on the flight and slept most of the trip. Dr. Gold had to wake him up after the plane landed back home.

Dr. Gold gently whispered, "We're here," to try to wake Prince up on the airplane. But Prince was sound asleep. He was sleeping like a log, and he didn't respond at all.

So, Dr. Gold tried again. He said a little bit louder, "Hey, Prince, it's time to get up." But still, nothing happened. Prince didn't move at all. He was like a rock. He obviously was still sound asleep and dreaming.

Dr. Gold was getting frustrated, so he gently shook Prince's shoulders and said loudly, "Come on, Prince! IT'S TIME TO GO!"

"Huh?" mumbled Prince as he slowly opened his eyes. He was still waking up and was totally confused. Prince had just been dreaming, and he had forgotten that he was on an airplane. It was still very early in the morning, so he was still half asleep. As Prince gradually stretched out his arms and legs, Dr. Gold was already unbuckling his seat belt and getting up from his seat.

After Prince rubbed the sleep out of his eyes, he realized that the plane had already landed, and he was very excited to be back home. He couldn't wait to see his best friend Ashley again. Since Ashley was not expecting him to be home today, Prince was planning to surprise her.

Prince undid his seatbelt, slowly stood up from his seat, and started to follow his dad off the plane. As Prince and Dr. Gold walked down the aisle toward the exit, a little old lady tapped Dr. Gold on the shoulder.

"Excuse me, sir," said the little old lady in a sweet voice. "Would you mind helping me get my purse in the container above us? As you can see, it's too high up, and I can't really reach."

"Of course," answered Dr. Gold. "No problem."

Dr. Gold opened the storage area above the little old lady and reached up to get her purse. Unfortunately, the woman had left her purse open and unzipped, so when Dr. Gold grabbed it, suddenly all of her stuff started to fall out of the bag. Dr. Gold didn't realize that the woman's purse had been left open, and everything in the purse was about to fall out all over the floor. It looked like it was going to make a huge mess.

Luckily, Prince had a special power to slow things down while he moved quickly. Prince saw everything falling out of the purse, but to him, it looked like everything was moving really, really slowly—like a snail. With his super-fast speed, Prince grabbed all the items that fell out of the woman's bag: sunglasses, a wallet, lipstick, keys, a pack of gum, a bottle of medicine, a hairbrush, and a granola bar. Not a single thing hit the floor. Prince's hands were full.

"Here you go," said Prince cheerfully to his dad as he handed him all of the stuff that fell out of the purse.

"Phew!" replied Dr. Gold as he put all the items back in the woman's purse. "Thank goodness you were here," he added with a huge sigh of relief.

"That would have been a big mess." Dr. Gold knew all about Prince's extraordinary power, so he wasn't surprised that Prince successfully caught everything.

Dr. Gold handed the little old lady her purse with all of her personal things back in it.

"Thank you," said the little old lady, who was a little surprised and confused. She didn't know that Prince had a special power, and she couldn't understand how Prince was able to catch everything that fell out of her purse without dropping a single item. She asked Dr. Gold, "How did he do that? How did that boy catch everything? It looked like everything was going to fall all over the floor. How was that possible?"

Dr. Gold just laughed and explained, "I guess my boy is very good at catching things. I think he maybe just got lucky." Dr. Gold actually knew that Prince didn't just get lucky. He understood that Prince had a unique ability and that it wasn't simply luck. But Dr. Gold did not want to tell the little old lady about the special power because it was Prince's secret.

"Oh, thank goodness," was all the little old lady could say in response. She still couldn't believe that Prince was able to move so fast and catch everything. She thought that maybe Prince really did just get lucky. Mostly, she was simply happy to have her purse back with everything still in it.

Dr. Gold and Prince followed the little old lady down the aisle and off of the plane. They then walked to the area where the suitcases come out at the airport.

When they got to the suitcase area, Prince saw a strange man across the hall waiting by himself. The man was wearing a heavy black wool coat, black jeans, black leather cowboy boots, a black cowboy hat, and dark sunglasses. It was weird to see somebody wearing a coat since it was still summer and very hot outside. And why was the guy wearing sunglasses inside the airport? Prince couldn't see the man's face very clearly, because the hat and sunglasses hid the man's face. But it seemed like the strange man was staring straight at Dr. Gold.

"Do you know that guy?" Prince asked his dad.

"What guy?" asked Dr. Gold.

Prince pointed to the place where the strange man was standing, but the man was already gone. Prince told his dad, "There was a guy right there. It looked like he was staring right at you. He was wearing a heavy black coat, and he had on a cowboy hat and dark sunglasses. Didn't you see him?"

"Nope," replied Dr. Gold. "But the guy does sound mysterious. I'm sure he was just some random traveler. I wouldn't worry about it," he added.

"Okay, I guess," said Prince, even though he really was still worried. There definitely was something mysterious about that man. Prince thought he looked very strange. The man looked like he was about to do something wrong. Prince was also starting to get a funny feeling in his tummy, which usually meant that something bad was going to happen. Sometimes when his friend, Ashley, was with him, she would get the same funny feeling in her stomach before something bad happened.

Meanwhile, Dr. Gold and Prince waited for their suitcases to come out of the big airport machine, called a conveyor belt. They watched as everyone else's bags dropped out of the machine and moved around in circles. One by one, each passenger would walk up and grab their suitcase off the conveyor belt. Dr. Gold and Prince just kept waiting. It was hard to tell which bags were theirs since almost all of the bags were black suitcases that looked exactly the same. Fortunately, Dr. Gold and Prince had planned in advance by tying red ribbons to the handles of their bags before they left

Washington, D.C., so that their suitcases would be easier to find at the airport.

"Look," said Dr. Gold as he pointed to a few suitcases with red ribbons circling around the conveyor belt machine. "Those are our bags."

"Yep," agreed Prince. "I'll get 'em." Prince ran and grabbed the suitcases with the red ribbons, and then he carefully checked the information tags that were tied to each bag to make sure they were the correct suitcases. The labels all had Dr. Gold's name, phone number, and home address written on them—they were definitely the right bags.

"Looks like we got everything," said Dr. Gold. "I'm going to go grab a luggage cart, so it'll be easier to carry all our stuff to the car. Why don't you wait here with our bags while I find the cart?"

"Okay," replied Prince. "No problem."

As Prince was waiting alone with the bags, the strange man wearing the heavy coat, cowboy hat, and sunglasses suddenly reappeared and walked up to Prince. Without saying a word, the man quickly grabbed one of Dr. Gold's suitcases and then disappeared with the suitcase. Prince could not believe what he had just seen. The mysterious man and one of the suitcases were gone. The man and the bag had just vanished.

Right after the man disappeared with the suitcase, Dr. Gold returned to Prince with the luggage cart to help carry all the bags to the car. Dr. Gold could tell that there was a problem by the look on Prince's face. Prince looked like something was bothering him. His mouth was wide open with his jaw hanging down. Prince was surprised and shocked. He looked like he had just seen a ghost.

"What's wrong?" Dr. Gold asked. "Are you okay?" He was very concerned with how Prince looked.

"Your, your, your suitcase," said Prince with a stutter. He was in such shock that it was hard for him to talk.

Dr. Gold looked at Prince and said, "It's okay. Calm down. Take a deeeeeep breath. Everything is fine. Tell me what happened."

Prince took a deep breath and held it for three long seconds. His dad was right—he did feel a little bit better. Prince then explained to his dad, "The strange man came back while you were gone. Then he grabbed your suitcase and just disappeared with it."

"Are you sure?" asked Dr. Gold. He then looked at their bags and noticed that one was missing.

"Yes, I'm certain," answered Prince. "The man and the suitcase just disappeared," he repeated. "I saw them, and then a second later, they were gone."

Dr. Gold was worried. He knew that Prince was a good boy and that he was telling the truth. Dr. Gold remembered the robbery last year at the bank where Ashley's dad, Mr. Pea, worked. A mysterious man called the 'Mystery Man' had helped Mr. Pea's boss, Mr. Wentworth, rob the bank using a machine that could make people invisible. Dr. Gold, Prince, Ashley, and Dr. Gold's friend, Agent Putty, all helped catch Mr. Wentworth and put him in jail. But nobody had ever captured the Mystery Man who had helped Mr. Wentworth steal the money. Dr. Gold was afraid that the strange man who had just stolen one of his suitcases might also be the same Mystery Man who helped rob the bank.

"Uh-oh," said Dr. Gold. "We better find that strange man. I have a feeling that it could be the same Mystery Man who robbed Mr. Pea's bank last year."

"Why would the Mystery Man want to take your suitcase?" asked Prince. "What was in it? What did he steal?" Prince knew that the Mystery Man robbed the bank to steal money. But he could not understand why the Mystery Man would want to steal his dad's suitcase. Prince didn't think the suitcase had a ton of money in it.

Dr. Gold looked at the remaining bags and started laughing. Prince was confused. Why was his dad laughing about his luggage getting stolen? So, he asked his dad, "What's so funny? Why are you laughing?"

Dr. Gold answered Prince's question, "It looks like the Mystery Man stole the wrong suitcase. He just stole the bag that had all of my dirty clothes, socks, and underwear in it." Dr. Gold thought it was hilarious. The Mystery Man didn't steal anything valuable. All he took was Dr. Gold's dirty laundry.

Prince started laughing too. He also thought it was pretty funny. Prince realized that the Mystery Man was going to be very disappointed when he realized the only things that he stole were dirty clothes, socks, and underwear.

"If he accidentally took the wrong suitcase," asked Prince, "then which one do you think he actually wanted to steal?"

Dr. Gold explained, "The Mystery Man probably thought he was stealing the suitcase that has my new special science equipment in it. But he must have taken the wrong bag by mistake since all the bags look alike." Dr. Gold laughed again. He was very happy that the Mystery Man had stolen the wrong bag.

"Why would he want to take your special science equipment?" asked Prince.

"That's a good question," replied Dr. Gold. "But I don't know the answer," he added. "He might have been trying to steal the special machine I invented to control electricity. My invention lets you do things like turn lights on and off, even if you're not in the same room as the lights. It's kind of like one big secret light switch that can control all the lights in a building at the same time."

Prince couldn't understand why anyone would need a machine like that, so he asked his dad, "What's the point of that machine? Why would anyone ever need a special light control switch?"

Dr. Gold responded, "I invented the machine to help save electricity. A lot of people who work in big buildings accidentally leave lights on at night, even after they've already gone home. Not only does that waste electricity, but it wastes money to pay for the electricity, and it is bad for the environment. Rather than having someone go around the entire building every night to make sure that each and every light switch is turned off, my special light control machine makes it easy to turn off all the lights at once."

Prince thought that sounded like a very cool invention. His dad was always coming up with clever devices to help people. But Prince still didn't understand why anyone would want to steal his dad's new creation. He asked, "Why do you think the Mystery Man wanted to take your machine?"

"Hmmm," mumbled Dr. Gold as he thought to himself for a couple of seconds. He then responded, "I don't know. I just don't understand why the Mystery Man would want this equipment."

Prince didn't know the answer either, but he guessed, "Maybe the Mystery Man is just lazy, and he doesn't like to go around his house flipping all the switches to turn off the lights at night."

"I guess that's possible," replied Dr. Gold. "But I just hope he wasn't trying to steal my equipment to do something else."

"What do you mean, 'something else?'" asked Prince.

"I don't know yet," responded Dr. Gold. "That's what I have to figure out," he added. "Since the Mystery Man is a bad guy, I hope he's not thinking about using a special light control machine to commit a crime. It's too bad he was able to disappear because now we can't follow him and stop him."

"I wish we had Ashley with us," said Prince. "She would be able to help us find the Mystery Man in the airport with her special power to see things that aren't there anymore."

"You're right," Dr. Gold agreed. "I think we're going to need all the help we can get to catch this Mystery Man, especially since he can make himself invisible. Let's get home as quickly as possible. I need to go to my laboratory and start working on a way to find this mysterious Mystery Man."

CHAPTER 2

WAFFLES WITH THE PEA FAMILY

After spending the entire summer apart, Prince was so excited that he would get to see Ashley again. He really, really missed her. Prince could not believe that it was already the end of summer and that he would be starting school in a few more days with Ashley. But Prince did not want to wait to see her at school. He wanted to see his best friend as quickly as possible.

It was still morning time when Prince got home from the airport with his dad. As soon as Dr. Gold parked at their house, Prince jumped out of the car. He was in a rush to go to Ashley's house. Prince ran up to his room and threw his suitcases on top of his bed. He immediately turned around and dashed back to the front door. Prince didn't even bother unpacking his dirty, smelly clothes from his bags after being gone for so many months.

As Prince was racing to the front door, he shouted to his dad, "Hey, Dad! Can I go down the hill to see Ashley?"

Dr. Gold yelled back from his room upstairs, "Okay, fine with me." He knew how excited Prince was to see his best friend, Ashley, and figured that Prince could always unpack and do his laundry later.

Prince was out the front door less than a second after his dad said he could go to Ashley's house. He ran as fast as he could down the long, curvy driveway from his enormous mansion at the top of the hill all the way to Ashley's tiny, little house at the bottom. After he made it down the road, he leaped up the stairs to the front porch of Ashley's house and knocked on the front door.

"Somebody's here!" shouted Ashley's little brother, Jacob, after he heard the knock. Jacob was with his parents, Mr. and Mrs. Pea, and Ashley in the kitchen, and they were just starting their breakfast since it was still fairly early in the morning.

"Who do you think it is?" asked Mr. Pea.

Prince knocked again and rang the doorbell.

"Well," replied Mrs. Pea, "somebody needs to go check."

Ashley, Jacob, and Mr. Pea didn't respond or move; they just stayed sitting at the table looking at Mrs. Pea.

"Fine," Mrs. Pea said with a huff, "I guess I'll do it." Mrs. Pea walked to the front door and saw through the window that Prince was there.

"Ashley and Jacob!" Mrs. Pea yelled toward the kitchen. "You might want to come and see who's here."

Ashley and Jacob looked at each other. They had no idea who it could be. They weren't expecting any visitors that morning. Ashley and Jacob had not seen Prince during the entire summer, and they didn't know that he had just returned from his big trip with his dad. They ran to the door to see who it was.

"IT'S PRINCE!" both Ashley and Jacob screamed with joy at the same time as soon as they saw him through the window by the front door. They were so excited to see him.

"Well, are you gonna make me wait out here all day, or are you going to let me in?" asked Prince while he was still standing outside the Pea house.

Ashley opened the door and ran straight to Prince to give him a huge hug. Prince could barely breathe because she was squeezing him so hard. Ashley had not seen him in a very long time, and she was so happy that her best friend was finally back.

"I want to hug Prince too," cried Jacob. "Ashley isn't letting me hug him," he said with a very whiny voice. Even though Prince was Ashley's friend, Jacob wished that Prince could have been his big brother. Jacob would always fight with his older sister Ashley about things like what to watch on TV or what toppings to get on pizza, but Jacob never argued with Prince.

"Come here, buddy," said Prince as he was standing outside hugging Ashley. "I've got room for both of you."

Jacob went up to Prince and also gave him a big hug. Prince just stood there for a minute with Ashley and Jacob hugging him.

"Hey," said Prince, "are you at least going to let me come in the house?"

Ashley and Jacob both laughed. "Of course," said Ashley. "Jacob, stop hugging Prince so he can come inside and hang out with us."

"All right," replied Jacob as he eventually let go of Prince.

Ashley and Jacob then went back inside the house, and Prince followed them.

"It's so great to see you again, Prince," said Mrs. Pea in a sweet voice as he entered the house.

"Thank you," replied Prince. "It's great to see all of you too. And I'm so happy to finally be back home."

"Welcome back, Prince!" added Mr. Pea from his seat at the kitchen table. "Why don't you come and join us for some of Mrs. Pea's delicious waffles?"

Before Prince could even answer, Jacob chimed in, "You have to stay for breakfast. Mom's waffles are the best. My mom even puts chocolate chips in them."

Everyone loved Mrs. Pea's cooking. She was especially good at adding chocolate chips to a bunch of her food creations. She made chocolate chip brownies, chocolate chip cookies, chocolate chip pancakes, chocolate chip bread, and—Jacob's favorite—chocolate chip waffles.

"Sounds like a great idea to me," said Prince. "You know how much I love to eat," he added. Prince could eat more than anyone. Even though he was not a big kid, Prince had a huge appetite, and his tummy never got full. Dr. Gold sometimes called Prince a human vacuum cleaner because he would eat every bit of food off his plate without leaving even a trace of any crumbs. The reason Prince was able to stay so skinny—even though he ate so much—was because of his special power. Usually, it would be unhealthy to eat as much as Prince. But Dr. Gold said it was okay since Prince needed all that food to energize his extraordinary ability—kind of like charging a cellphone.

As Prince followed Ashley and Jacob back to the kitchen table, he got more and more excited to eat the chocolate chip waffles that Mrs. Pea had made. He could smell the delicious scent of the waffles all the way down the hall. Mr. Pea and Mrs. Pea each had one waffle on their plate, and Ashley and Jacob each had two waffles. Prince took five waffles and put them all on his plate.

"Looks like you're still the hungriest person around," Mr. Pea said to Prince after he saw how full Prince's plate was.

"This is just to start," replied Prince. "It's all that could fit on my plate for my first round. I'll be ready for some more as soon as I finish these."

"Well, I guess it's a good thing I made lots of extras," said Mrs. Pea cheerfully. She took it as a nice compliment that everyone loved her cooking so much.

Mr. Pea then added, "Prince, don't forget to eat all your broccoli first."

"Wait, what did you say?" asked Prince. He wasn't sure that he heard Mr. Pea correctly. Did Mr. Pea really just tell him to eat broccoli for breakfast? Prince was very confused. Who eats broccoli for breakfast? He didn't even see any broccoli on the kitchen table. What was Mr. Pea talking about? So, he asked Mr. Pea to clear up the confusion, "Did you just say broccoli?"

"Would you prefer green beans?" Mr. Pea responded to Prince.

"Huh?" replied Prince with a confused look on his face. Why would Mr. Pea ask him if he wanted green beans with his breakfast? Who eats broccoli or green beans for breakfast? It sounded like the strangest breakfast that Prince had ever heard of.

Mr. Pea then started laughing. He could tell that Prince was very confused.

Ashley came to the rescue and explained to Prince, "Don't worry, Prince. My dad is just kidding with you. He's such a jokester. He wasn't being serious."

"Oh, phew," replied Prince. "Thank goodness!" Prince was glad it was a joke. He certainly did not want to eat any broccoli or green beans with his delicious chocolate chip waffle breakfast. Broccoli and green beans with waffles sounded disgusting.

"I have a joke too," said Jacob. He wanted to be funny, just like his dad.

"Okay, buddy," said Prince. "Let's hear your joke."

"Knock, knock," said Jacob.

"Who's there?" asked Prince. He knew Jacob liked to tell knock-knock jokes.

"Soup," replied Jacob.

"Soup who?" asked Prince.

"SUPERHEROES!" yelled Jacob as he started laughing at his own joke. He thought his joke was hilarious, even though nobody else at the table was really laughing.

"Good one," said Prince. He didn't honestly think Jacob's joke was funny, but he laughed a little bit to make Jacob feel good about his joke. Prince was always thinking about how to be nice to other people.

"All right," said Mrs. Pea, "that's enough jokes for now." She knew that Jacob would keep telling knock-knock jokes all morning unless she told him to stop.

Ashley then asked Prince, "So, what do you want to do today? Remember, this is the last week of summer vacation before school starts."

"Well," replied Prince, "I thought I would just stay home alone today and play by myself."

Ashley was very disappointed after hearing Prince's answer. She couldn't believe that he didn't want to hang out with her and do something together. It seemed like Prince didn't miss her as much as she missed him, which made her very unhappy. She said to Prince with a sad voice, "But I thought you would want to hang out with me today."

Prince smiled and chuckled. "I was just kidding," he replied. "You should know better. Of course, I want to hang out with you."

"Oh, phew," said Ashley with a sigh of relief and a little laugh now that she knew Prince was joking. "That's great!" she added. Ashley felt happy again. She also felt a little silly for not realizing that Prince was just kidding.

"Why don't we go over to my house after breakfast?" asked Prince.

Ashley then asked her mom and dad, "Can I go to Prince's house?" She then added in her nicest and sweetest voice, "Pleeeaaassse."

"I am sure you physically *can* go to Prince's house," answered Mr. Pea while emphasizing the word 'can.' "But what is the correct way to ask for permission to do something?"

Ashley remembered that when you ask for permission to do something or go somewhere, you were supposed to use the word 'may' instead of 'can.' So, she tried again, "Please, *may* I go to Prince's house?"

Mr. Pea answered, "It's fine with me, but only if it's all right with your mom."

"I guess it's okay with me," replied Mrs. Pea. "It's your last week of summer vacation, so you kids should have some fun before school starts."

"YAY!" yelled Prince and Ashley at the same time.

"What about me?" Jacob asked. He was jealous that Prince and Ashley always got to play together without him.

"You're not invited," explained Ashley. "Only I'm allowed to go to Prince's house. Prince is my friend, not yours."

Jacob didn't like Ashley's answer at all. He looked like he was about to cry. He loved when Prince came over to his house, and he didn't understand why he wasn't allowed to go to Prince's house with Ashley.

"ASHLEY – JULIA – PEA," said Mr. Pea slowly with an angry voice. "That was not a nice thing to say to your little brother. You need to apologize and say you're sorry."

"But why?" asked Ashley. She knew her dad was very serious whenever he called her by her full name. And she didn't think she had done anything wrong.

"What you said was very mean to Jacob," explained Mr. Pea. "That really hurt his feelings."

"But I didn't mean to hurt his feelings," replied Ashley. She was telling the truth. Ashley didn't realize that she had said anything wrong. Prince was her best friend, and they never included Jacob when they played together at Prince's house.

"Sweetie, I know you weren't trying to be mean," said Mrs. Pea to Ashley. "You just need to find a nicer way to explain things. You need to be more careful about the words you use, so you don't hurt people's feelings."

"How should I explain it better?" Ashley asked.

Mrs. Pea suggested, "How about saying something like, 'I'm sorry, Jacob. Prince is still your friend, but sometimes Prince and I like to just play by ourselves. It doesn't mean that we don't like you. It just means that sometimes we need time for only big kids. Don't worry. Prince will be back here to play with you soon.'"

"That does sound a lot nicer," agreed Mr. Pea.

"I guess I understand," admitted Ashley. She did not mean to hurt Jacob's feelings, and she learned that there was a kinder way she could have explained things to Jacob. "Sorry, Jacob," she said to her little brother.

Jacob still looked a little sad. "Well," he said to his parents, "is there anything else special I can do today since Ashley gets to go to Prince's house?"

"That does sound fair," replied Mr. Pea.

"Why don't we go to the library together and pick out some new books for you to read?" suggested Mrs. Pea.

"Yay!" Jacob replied. "That sounds good." Jacob loved books, just like Prince and Ashley. He was sad that he couldn't go to Prince's house to play. But Jacob was happy that he would at least get some new books to read.

Prince quickly finished off the five chocolate chip waffles on his plate, and then he ate two more. After he finished his seventh waffle, he said, "Thank you, Mr. and Mrs. Pea, for breakfast. It was delicious."

"I'm glad you enjoyed all those waffles," replied Mrs. Pea.

"May Prince and I please be excused so we can go to Prince's house now that we're both done with breakfast?" asked Ashley very politely. This time she remembered to ask for permission using the word 'may' and not 'can.'

"That was excellent manners," Mrs. Pea observed. "Yes," she responded, "you may both be excused."

Mr. Pea added, "Just put your dishes and silverware in the sink first. You don't want to leave a mess that someone else has to clean up."

"Okay," replied Prince and Ashley at the same time.

Prince and Ashley both got up from the kitchen table and started cleaning up their stuff. As they were putting everything in the sink, Jacob asked Prince, "Why was the cowboy guy from my dad's bank with you at the airport?"

"What?" asked Prince. He was a bit confused. What was Jacob talking about? How could Jacob know about anyone who was with him at the airport? Jacob was never even at the airport, and Prince had never told him about any guy at the airport.

"The man with the cowboy hat," replied Jacob. "He had a big coat and sunglasses, and he took your dad's suitcase."

Prince could not believe what Jacob had just said. Jacob had perfectly described the strange man who stole his dad's bag at the airport. But Jacob was never at the airport. How could he possibly know about the Mystery Man and the suitcase?

"How do you know about that guy?" Prince asked Jacob.

"Because," answered Jacob, "I thought his big black cowboy hat looked kind of funny. I saw him at my dad's bank when the police were there for the robbery last year, and then I knew it was the same guy at the airport with you this morning."

"But," Prince questioned, "how did you know it was the same guy when you weren't even with me at the airport?"

Jacob thought for a moment, and then he answered Prince's question, "I knew it was the same guy because I'm smart."

Prince did not think Jacob's answer made any sense. He was getting frustrated with Jacob. What did being smart have to do with seeing a guy at the airport, especially when Jacob was never even at the airport?

Ashley was just as confused as Prince. She knew her brother hadn't been to the airport, and Prince had never mentioned anything about a man with a coat, hat, and sunglasses. She didn't understand how Jacob could know about the strange man.

"Being smart doesn't explain anything," Ashley said to Jacob. "How could you just know something without actually being there?"

"Because I'm smart," repeated Jacob. "I told you that I'm smart, and that's why I know things."

Ashley was not satisfied with her little brother's answer. She was getting frustrated with Jacob too. It still did not make any sense. She tried asking him the same question a different way, "If you weren't at the airport, then how did you *see* the guy at the airport?" She said the word 'see' very slowly, clearly, and loudly.

Jacob paused because he did not know how to answer Ashley's question. Sometimes he just knew stuff, but he didn't know how he knew those things. He tried to answer her question, "Because I saw it in my head. That's how I see things when I'm not there. I see them in my head."

Prince and Ashley did not understand how Jacob could simply see things in his head. They were both very confused, and neither of them had ever heard about anyone seeing things in their head. How could someone see something if they weren't using their eyes?

Prince finally said to Ashley, "I think we may need to talk to my dad about Jacob. My dad is a genius scientist, so maybe he can help explain it better to us."

Ashley thought to herself for a second and then said to Prince, "What if Jacob has his own special power? He might have a super secret special power just like us."

"Hmmm," replied Prince as he wondered if it was possible. "That would be kind of cool," he added.

"Let's go see what your dad has to say," said Ashley.

So, Prince and Ashley finished cleaning up the kitchen table, and then they ran up the hill to Prince's house. They had some important questions about Jacob that they needed to ask Dr. Gold.

CHAPTER 3

THE GARDEN AT THE GOLD HOUSE

By the time Prince and Ashley finished running up the long, winding road to Prince's house, they were totally out of breath. It was a very steep hill. Ashley could feel her heart beating very fast, and she could tell that Prince was also tired from the run.

When they entered the house, Prince shouted, "Dad, I'm home! Ashley's with me."

But Dr. Gold didn't respond.

"Where's your dad?" asked Ashley.

"He's probably working on one of his secret government science projects downstairs in his laboratory," replied Prince. "He's trying to figure out how to catch the Mystery Man who robbed your dad's bank last year and then stole my dad's suitcase at the airport this morning."

Ashley looked around the house. She was using her super secret special power to see things that used to be there but weren't there anymore. She looked at the door leading down to Dr. Gold's laboratory in the basement.

"Actually," said Ashley, "I don't think your dad is down there anymore."

"How do you know?" asked Prince.

"Because of my special power," answered Ashley. "I could see that he left the basement a little while ago. I saw his shadowy figure head to the glass doors at the back of your house—the ones that lead outside to your backyard."

"Oh yeah," replied Prince. "I should have known you were using your special power. It sure does come in handy." Prince thought for a second and then added, "My dad must be outside working on his garden."

"Well," said Ashley, "let's go outside and see him."

Prince and Ashley walked down the long hallway to the back of the house, opened the big sliding glass doors, and stepped outside onto a huge wooden patio. From the deck, they could see the enormous lawn that stretched out behind the mansion. The yard was gigantic—like a park or a golf course. It looked like you could fit a dozen soccer fields on it. And, at the far end of the backyard, there was the most beautiful display of flowers that Ashley had ever seen. There were thousands of flowers—all different types and colors. The entire front of the garden was covered with large, pretty roses, which were Ashley's favorite type of flower.

"There he is," said Prince as he pointed to his dad at the back of the garden. Dr. Gold was using a hose to water some of the flowers.

"Hi, Dr. Gold!" shouted Ashley as she walked toward the garden.

"Hi, Dad!" said Prince.

Dr. Gold was startled. He was not expecting Prince to return home so soon from the Pea house.

"Hi, kids!" Dr. Gold yelled back.

Prince and Ashley walked along a narrow, pebbled path that led through the yard to the beautiful garden where Dr. Gold was watering the plants.

Right as Prince and Ashley walked up, Dr. Gold yelled, "Think fast!" He then pointed his hose right at Prince and Ashley. Water was about to spray all over them.

Luckily, Prince was able to use his special power to grab Ashley and move both of them out of the way of the water before even a single drop hit them. Without Prince's extraordinary ability to move so quickly, they would have been drenched. All of their clothes would have been soaking wet.

Even though Ashley knew that Prince had a special power, she was still surprised that he was able to move her out of the way in time. She had seen Dr. Gold point the hose at her, and she had even seen the water coming out of the hose. But the next thing she knew, Prince was holding her in a different spot in the garden, and she was watching the water hit the ground right in the place where she used to be standing.

"Thanks for keeping me from getting wet," Ashley said to Prince.

"No problem," replied Prince.

"Great job using your special power," Dr. Gold told Prince.

"It was easy," admitted Prince. "After all my practice, I'm really good at using my special power."

Dr. Gold liked to help Prince and Ashley practice using their super secret special powers. He wanted to make sure that Prince and Ashley learned how to use their powers perfectly so that they could become great detectives and help catch bad guys. Dr. Gold said to them, "Maybe you both are finally good enough with your powers to help me catch the Mystery Man."

"I know that I'm ready," responded Prince. He was absolutely sure that he was perfect at using his powers. Prince had been practicing his powers almost every day.

"I guess I'm ready too," added Ashley, but she was not as certain as Prince. She also had practiced using her powers almost every day, but she was a little scared that the Mystery Man might try to hurt her. She was glad that Prince and Dr. Gold would be around to help protect her.

"We are so lucky that you two kids have your special powers," said Dr. Gold. "I don't think we would be able to catch the Mystery Man without them."

Ashley then remembered what Jacob had said about the Mystery Man, even though he was never at the airport. She told Dr. Gold, "There might be another kid with special powers who could also help us."

"What are you talking about?" asked Dr. Gold. "Who else can help us?" Dr. Gold only knew about Prince and Ashley having special powers. He didn't know any other people who had such unique abilities.

"Well," replied Ashley, "my little brother, Jacob, might have a special power too."

"That's right," agreed Prince. He then explained to his dad, "Somehow Jacob knew about the Mystery Man stealing your suitcase at the airport, even though I never told him anything about it. Jacob said that he saw the Mystery Man at the airport, but Jacob was never actually at the airport.

"He also said that he saw the same Mystery Man at our dad's bank after the big robbery last year," added Ashley.

"Hmmm," was all Dr. Gold could say. He wondered to himself, *How could Jacob possibly have seen the Mystery Man at the airport without being there? What extraordinary power could he have?* Dr. Gold just stood there in front of Prince and Ashley without saying anything. He was deep in thought.

Ashley got tired of waiting for Dr. Gold to say something. So, she asked him, "How was Jacob able to see things without being there?" Jacob's special power didn't make any sense to Ashley. Even though Ashley had an extraordinary ability, she didn't understand how Jacob's power worked. Ashley could see things that used to be there with her power, but she had to actually be in the same room to see those things that already happened. How could Jacob see anything without ever really being there?

"Hmmm," Dr. Gold said again. He was still wondering about Jacob's unique power. Dr. Gold had never heard anything about an ability to see things without being there. It sounded like Jacob had an extraordinary power that was different from both Prince and Ashley. Dr. Gold had read thousands of books about people having special abilities. But none of those books described anything like Jacob's power. Even though he was a brilliant scientist, Dr. Gold just didn't know how to explain Jacob's power. He didn't understand how it worked.

After thinking quietly to himself for what seemed like a pretty long time, Dr. Gold finally said, "I need to talk with Jacob. I have to find out more about his special power. Why don't you bring Jacob over here with you next time so I can do some scientific tests to figure out his special power?"

"Jacob would love that!" exclaimed Ashley. "He always wants to come over here to play with Prince and me. He is going to be so excited."

"Wouldn't it be so cool if Jacob had his own special power?" said Prince. "We could be like three superhero kids who use their powers to stop bad guys."

But Ashley was afraid of bad guys, and she was scared about getting hurt by them. "I don't want to be a superhero," responded Ashley. "I just want to be a normal kid." Ashley wasn't scared about being a detective and helping to solve crimes, but being a superhero sounded very scary to her.

"Ashley's right," replied Dr. Gold. "I don't want you kids to be superheroes. That is way too dangerous. I only want you to use your special powers to help me do detective work when I am with you. Even though you have special powers, you are still kids, and you can still get hurt."

"But," argued Prince, "I move too fast for anyone to hurt me. Nobody can catch me."

Without saying a word, Dr. Gold scooped up a handful of wet, muddy dirt from the garden, and then he threw it at Prince while he wasn't paying attention. Unlike with the water hose earlier, this time, Dr. Gold did not warn Prince by saying, 'think fast.' Prince did not see the dirt coming at him after Dr. Gold threw it, so he was not ready to use his special power to avoid it. The disgusting and dirty goop of mud got all over Prince's face and hair.

"YUCK!" yelled Prince as he started using his hands to wipe the mess off his face. "Why'd you do that?" he cried. Prince was definitely going to need a shower later to clean off all the dirty mess.

"I had to teach you a lesson," replied Dr. Gold. "I wanted to show you that your special power can't stop everything. Someone could surprise you when you're not expecting it. You need to learn that even with a special power, a bad guy still might be able to hurt you."

"I guess I understand now," admitted Prince. "Maybe my special power can't stop everything." Prince realized that he wasn't really a superhero and that bad guys actually could hurt him.

Dr. Gold reminded Prince and Ashley, "Catching criminals is important. But my number one rule is that safety is the most important thing," He then asked, "If we're going to work together as detectives, then do you both promise to always follow all of my rules when using your special powers?"

"Yes," answered both Prince and Ashley at the same time.

"Sounds good," replied Dr. Gold. "Now that that's settled, why don't you two go play and enjoy your final days of summer vacation? Don't forget to bring Jacob by one of these days so we can do some scientific testing to figure out his special power."

"Okay, we'll remember," answered Prince. "Bye, Dad," he added.

"Bye, Dr. Gold," said Ashley.

"See you later, kids," responded Dr. Gold. He then went back to watering his plants with his hose and working on his garden.

Prince and Ashley turned around and started walking back along the narrow, pebbled path through the garden to the house.

"Why don't I show you all of the cool books that I read while I was in Washington, D.C.?" suggested Prince to Ashley. "I know you'll want to borrow some of them."

"Sure," replied Ashley. She knew that a lot of kids would just want to watch TV or play video games. But her favorite thing to do was to read books. She was so happy that she found someone like Prince, who also liked to read books as much as her. Ashley then reminded Prince, "But first, you are going to need to go wash all the mud off your face and hair that your dad threw on you."

Prince laughed and responded, "Yep, he sure got me good." Prince then ran to the bathroom to wash up as quickly as possible so he could go back to hanging out with his best friend, Ashley.

CHAPTER 4

WALKING TO SCHOOL

It was Monday morning, and the bright sun was rising up in the sky. Summer vacation was officially done. Ashley woke up drowsy because she had stayed up late the night before reading one of the awesome books that Prince had let her borrow. Even though she was still really tired when her alarm clock went off, she jumped out of bed as soon as the alarm started beeping. Ashley hated that darn beeping sound. She had been begging her parents to buy her an alarm clock that plays music when it goes off, but her dad said Ashley would have to wait until Christmas. She didn't want to have to wait until Christmas. That beeping sound made her start every morning in a bad mood. It was so annoying. Sometimes her parents just didn't understand.

Ashley brushed her teeth, washed her face, and then got dressed for school. She was able to get dressed extremely quickly because she had already set aside her clothes for school on the previous day. Before she went to bed, Ashley and her mom had spent more than an hour trying to pick out the perfect outfit for the first day of school. Ashley wanted to look as pretty as possible for her first day back to school after summer vacation. She told her mom that she wanted to look pretty for all her friends, but the truth was that Ashley really only cared about looking beautiful for Prince.

After Ashley finished getting ready, she ran down the stairs to the kitchen to have breakfast. Jacob was already there with her mom and dad. Her parents were always awake before her, and they always started the morning drinking large mugs filled to the brim with coffee. Ashley could smell the strong scent of the coffee coming from the kitchen, and she couldn't understand why her parents liked such a gross and disgusting drink. She had once tried a sip of her parents' coffee, but she thought it was horrible and that it tasted like dirt.

"Good morning, sweetheart," said Mrs. Pea as soon as Ashley arrived.

"Good morning, sleepyhead," added Mr. Pea.

Ashley had a big yawn, and then she slowly replied, "Hi, everyone."

Jacob didn't say anything. He was too busy eating his cereal.

Ashley grabbed herself a bowl and spoon, and then she sat down at the kitchen table. The milk, a box of Life cereal, and a box of Cheerios were already on the table. Ashley's favorite cereals were sugar cereals, but her parents only allowed Jacob and her to have them on special occasions. Mr. and Mrs. Pea had a rule that Ashley and Jacob could only pick out cereals at the supermarket with less than seven grams of sugar per serving, and it was very tough to find a good cereal with such little sugar.

"Are you excited to be going back to school?" Mr. Pea asked Ashley.

"Yeah, I guess," answered Ashley. Ashley wasn't really that excited about school, but she was thrilled that Prince was now back in town and that she would get to see him every day at school.

"I'm excited!" shouted Jacob. Today was going to be Jacob's first day of elementary school. He was starting kindergarten.

"We know you're excited," replied Mrs. Pea. "You have been talking about kindergarten all summer," she added.

"Don't forget to take care of your little brother," Mr. Pea reminded Ashley. "Remember, the first day at a new school can be pretty scary."

"I'm not scared," Jacob informed everyone. "I'm brave."

"Yes, of course, you're brave," agreed Mr. Pea. "You're going to have a great day. I just know it. But Ashley needs to remember that a big sister's job is to take care of her younger brother. That's an important part of being in a family."

"Okay, fine," agreed Ashley with a huff. Secretly, she was not happy that Jacob was going to the same school as her. Ashley knew that she was supposed to love her brother, but sometimes he could be an annoying little pest. At least, she wouldn't have to see him too much at school. The kindergartners had a different recess and lunch schedule than the rest of the grades, and they even had their own playground. The only time Ashley was actually going to have to spend with Jacob was the walk to and from school.

Ashley and Jacob finished eating their breakfast while Mrs. Pea made their lunches. Jacob was happy to eat almost anything, but Ashley was very picky about her food. She only really liked to eat turkey sandwiches with cheese for her school lunch. But there couldn't be too much turkey or too much cheese, or else she wouldn't like it. Mrs. Pea knew how to make a perfect sandwich for Ashley every time. Once, Mr. Pea tried to make Ashley's sandwich for her lunch, but he overloaded it with turkey, and then a bunch of the turkey pieces spilled out onto her lap when she tried to eat the sandwich later at school. Even though Ashley was old enough to know how to make her own lunch, her mom said that she actually liked to do it for her. Also, her mom was afraid that if Ashley got to make her own lunch, she would pack way too much junk food and snacks.

"Here you go," said Mrs. Pea as she handed Ashley and Jacob their lunch bags.

"Thanks, Mom," replied Ashley.

Jacob didn't say anything. He just grabbed his blue and red lunch box, which had pictures of superhero guys all over it.

"Don't forget your manners," Mr. Pea reminded Jacob.

"Oops, I forgot," responded Jacob. "Thank you, Mom," he added.

As Ashley and Jacob finished their breakfast, Ashley asked her mom and dad, "Would it be okay for Jacob to go with me to Prince's house after school?" Ashley remembered that Dr. Gold wanted to see Jacob in order to figure out how Jacob's special power worked.

Jacob was so excited. He couldn't believe that Ashley was going to let him go over to Prince's house with her. Jacob had always wanted to go there to play with Prince. "YAY!" he shouted. "Please, Mom. Please, Dad. Can I go?" he begged.

"You mean, may I go?" Mr. Pea corrected Jacob since it was not correct to use the word 'can' in English to ask permission.

"Oh yeah," responded Jacob, as he asked again, "Please, *may* I go with Ashley to Prince's house after school?" He emphasized the word 'may' to show his parents that he was using the correct manners and grammar.

"Well," replied Mrs. Pea, "if it's all right with Prince and Dr. Gold, then it's okay with me."

"Just make sure you do all of your homework first," added Mr. Pea. "You know the rules."

"Don't worry," Ashley informed her parents, "there's no homework on the first day of school."

She added, "Usually, the teachers barely give any homework for the entire first week of school."

"Okay then," replied Mr. Pea. "I guess you two can go have fun at Prince's house after school."

"YAY!" yelled Ashley and Jacob at the same time.

Ashley looked at the clock and then said to Jacob, "We better hurry up and go outside now. Prince should be here any minute."

"Okay," replied Jacob. Usually, Jacob didn't like to listen to Ashley, and he hated it when she told him what to do. But Jacob remembered that he was supposed to be an excellent listener with Ashley and not argue with her. His mom and dad had told him that he had to follow Ashley's rules when they walked to and from school, or else he wouldn't be allowed to walk together with Prince and Ashley.

Ashley and Jacob went outside and waited patiently on the porch in front of their house for Prince. They could see Prince running down the hill from his house to meet them. He was racing as fast as he could.

As Prince ran up to the porch, Ashley asked him, "Why don't you just leave your house a little earlier in the morning? That way, you won't always have to run so fast not to be late."

Prince waited for a second to catch his breath after his fast run and then replied, "But I like to run. My dad says that every time I practice running, it makes me an even faster runner."

"Why do you need to be such a fast runner?" asked Jacob.

"Because," answered Prince, "that way I can beat you in a race, even if I give you a big head start."

"Can we race to school?" asked Jacob. He was pretty excited. He loved running races, especially with Prince.

"Not today," answered Ashley. "I didn't wear my running sneakers today. The only shoes that matched my outfit were my pretty pink and sparkly slip-on shoes. And they are too slippery to run in."

"Okay," Jacob responded with a sad voice. He was disappointed, but he knew that he was supposed to listen to his big sister.

"Well, we better get going to school," mentioned Prince. "We don't want to be late on our first day."

Jacob, Ashley, and Prince started walking together to school. There was only room for two people to walk next to each other on the sidewalk. So, Prince and Ashley walked side by side, and

Jacob walked in front of them. Jacob was happy to be in front because he always liked to be the leader.

Right before they all got to the school, Ashley shouted, "JACOB, STOP!"

Jacob stopped immediately. He was a little confused. Why did Ashley want him to stop so suddenly? They were all on the sidewalk. He didn't see anything dangerous—like a car coming. He turned around and asked Ashley, "Why do I need to stop?"

"Because," Ashley warned him, "those are three big, awful bullies ahead of us. Those three bullies like to pick on all the little kids and steal their stuff. Even though Prince can protect us, they still might be mean and call us names. It's better just to wait for them to leave so that we can avoid them."

Ashley hated the three bullies. Before Prince started protecting her, they used to call her 'Pee Girl'—like the pee from when you go to the bathroom—just because her last name was Pea, even though her last name was spelled like the vegetable, pea, and not the bathroom kind of pee. The three bullies once even tried to steal a book that Ashley was reading and light it on fire, but Prince had saved her and the book by using his special power to slow things down while he moved very quickly.

"Okay," Jacob replied to Ashley without arguing, "I'll wait here with you." He was on his best behavior with Ashley. Jacob knew that his parents would be very proud of him for listening to Ashley and not complaining.

"Ashley's right," added Prince. "I know I can stop them from hurting us, but it's easier to avoid a fight rather than win a fight."

Jacob looked at the three bullies—they were all much, much bigger and stronger than Prince. Jacob couldn't understand how Prince could possibly protect him from the three big bullies because he didn't know that Prince had an extraordinary power to make things move slowly while he moved quickly.

As Jacob, Ashley, and Prince were waiting on the sidewalk, the bullies watched the younger children get dropped off at school by their parents. The biggest one of the bullies, Brody, then walked over to one little boy as soon as his parents' car drove away. He grabbed the boy by his shirt collar, and it looked like he was going to hurt the little boy.

Jacob saw all of this happening. He pointed to the little boy and exclaimed, "That boy needs help. I know him. His name is Luke, and he's my friend from preschool. It looks like that big bully is hurting him." Jacob was worried about his friend. He wanted to help him, but he didn't know what he could do.

"Don't worry," replied Prince, "I'll take care of it."

Jacob glanced over at Ashley with a concerned look on his face, but Ashley simply smiled back at him calmly. She then said, "Just wait a second. With Prince's help, Luke won't have to worry about the bullies bothering him any longer."

Jacob believed Prince and Ashley, even though he didn't know how Prince could stop the bullies. There were three bullies, and Prince was only one person. Also, the three bullies were all so much bigger and stronger than Prince. Jacob thought to himself, *What could Prince possibly do to help?*

Suddenly, Brody was lying on the ground with the other two bullies piled on top of him. It all happened in the blink of an eye. The three bullies were all trying to get up, but they somehow all seemed to be stuck together. Brody's belt had mysteriously come off his pants and become tied around the three bullies' legs. Every time one of the bullies tried to move, he would end up tripping and kicking the other two bullies.

While Brody and the other two bullies were struggling on the ground, Luke ran to his classroom before the bullies could stand up and get him. Jacob just stood there on the sidewalk with Prince and Ashley staring at the bullies. He couldn't believe it. One minute the three bullies were picking on his friend Luke and the next minute, they were all lying on the ground tied together by a belt.

Prince and Ashley stood next to Jacob and laughed. They didn't seem surprised at all. They were the only ones who knew the real secret about what had just happened to the three bullies. Nobody else could tell that Prince had used his special power to slow things down while he moved quickly.

After the three bullies struggled on the ground for a couple of minutes, Brody finally realized that his belt was sticking them all together. He reached down and untied the loop so the bullies could all get up. After the three bullies freed themselves from the belt, Brody stood up and noticed Prince standing on the sidewalk. Brody got a worried look on his face because he was scared of Prince. The three bullies didn't know how Prince did it, but he was always able to stop them from doing bad things.

Brody yelled to the other two bullies, "It's Prince. Let's get out of here." Brody started running away, and the other two bullies quickly followed him.

"Phew!" exclaimed Ashley with a sigh of relief. "Thank goodness they're finally gone."

Jacob couldn't figure out why Brody was afraid of Prince. He didn't realize that Prince had just saved his friend, Luke, from the bullies. Prince had moved too fast for Jacob to even notice. He asked Prince, "Why are the bullies afraid of you? Why did they run away? How did they end up on the ground?"

"Those are all good questions," answered Prince. "Why don't I explain it to you at my house after school?"

"Okay, I guess," replied Jacob. He really wanted to know the answers right then, but he knew he had to be patient. He didn't want to argue with Prince and ruin his chance to go to Prince's house after school.

"Hey, we better hurry and get to class," suggested Ashley. "The tardy bell is about to ring."

CHAPTER 5

FIRST DAY OF SCHOOL

Prince and Ashley walked Jacob straight to his new kindergarten classroom. Ashley knew where it was because she had the same class and the same teacher when she was in kindergarten. The classroom looked exactly the same to Ashley. It hadn't changed in years. There was a huge chalkboard in the front of the class. On top of the chalkboard were the letters of the alphabet painted in big, bright red and blue colors. Several posters of farm animals were hanging on the wall at the back of the room. On one side of the room was a shelf full of cubbies, where the kids could put their backpacks and jackets. On the other side of the room was an enormous bookshelf full of hundreds of books. In the middle of the classroom were five round tables. Each table had four chairs around it, and most of the chairs already had kids sitting in them by the time Jacob had arrived.

As they walked in the room, Jacob recognized a few other kids from his preschool class, but a lot of the kids he had never seen before. Jacob's friend, Luke, was already sitting down in a chair at the front of the classroom. Luke waved to Jacob as he walked into the room, and Jacob waved back.

The kindergarten teacher, Miss Darling, greeted Jacob right away, "Welcome to your new kindergarten class. I'm your new teacher, Miss Darling."

Jacob was a little bit shy around new people. He replied in a hushed whisper-like voice, "Hi."

Miss Darling continued, "I know that you must be Jacob because I recognized your big sister, Ashley, as soon as you entered the room. Ashley was one of my favorite, most well-behaved students when she was in kindergarten, and I just know that you're going to be a great student too. I think we're going to have a wonderful school year together. I already have a seat picked out just for you right over here by our class hamsters, Ruby and Crystal."

Jacob simply smiled and didn't say anything back because he was still acting a little bit shy.

Miss Darling led Jacob to a seat at the table right in the front of the class—next to Luke and by the big hamster cage. Jacob was happy that he got to sit next to his friend, Luke, and he was very excited to sit next to the hamsters. Ashley had already told him that every kid in kindergarten gets a turn to take the hamsters home for a weekend. And Jacob couldn't wait until it was his turn.

After Jacob sat down, Ashley said, "See you later, Jacob." She left Jacob in the classroom and turned around to go to her class.

"See you, buddy," added Prince right after Ashley's comment. Prince was in a different class than Ashley, but he always liked to first walk Ashley to her room before going to his own classroom.

"Bye!" replied Jacob as Prince and Ashley left the room.

Jacob was sad to see Prince and Ashley leave, but he was excited to be in his new classroom. Some of the kids in the kindergarten class were crying because they missed their moms and dads—but not Jacob. He told his parents that he was brave, and Jacob wanted to show everyone that he wasn't scared to be in kindergarten.

When the tardy bell finally rang, Miss Darling told all the kindergarten students to stand up.

Everyone listened to her, even the kids who were crying. Miss Darling then said in a friendly, sweet voice with a big smile on her face, "Welcome, all you wonderful new kindergarten students. Every morning after the final tardy bell rings, we stand up, turn toward the flag in the front of the class, put our hands over our hearts, and then we say the Pledge of Allegiance." Miss Darling paused for a second and then asked, "Does anyone know the words to the Pledge?"

All of the kids in the class, except for Jacob, had blank looks on their faces. Jacob was the only one who understood what Miss Darling was talking about. None of the other kids knew what the Pledge of Allegiance was.

"I DO!" shouted Jacob. He was so proud of himself for knowing all the words, and he wanted to show off how smart he was.

Miss Darling was not happy that Jacob had shouted out the answer, so she informed him, "In kindergarten, we don't yell out answers. If you would like to answer a question, the rule is that you need to raise your hand first and then wait for me to call on you."

Jacob was so embarrassed. He was trying to be on his best behavior for school, and he didn't want to get in trouble on his first day. He thought that Miss Darling was angry with him, and he felt like he was about to cry.

Miss Darling could tell by Jacob's sad-looking face that he felt bad about breaking the rules. So, she said to him in a sweet and calm voice, "It's all right, Jacob. You didn't know the rule, so you aren't in trouble. Now you know how to do it right next time." She then said, "Let's try again. Does anyone know the words to the Pledge?"

Jacob now understood the rule that he wasn't supposed to shout out the answer, so he raised his hand instead. All the other kids in class just turned at stared at Jacob.

"Yes, Jacob," said Miss Darling. "Do you know all the words?"

Jacob replied, "Yes, I'm really smart, and I know lots of things."

Miss Darling chuckled a little. "Well, then," she responded, "why don't you go ahead and say the words to the Pledge of Allegiance? You get to be the class leader this morning."

Jacob smiled with a huge grin on his face. He was so happy to be the class leader on the first day of school. Jacob loved to be a leader. With a very loud and clear voice, Jacob said the words perfectly, "I pledge allegiance to the flag of the United States of America, and to the republic for which it stands, one nation under God, indivisible, with liberty and justice for all."

"That was excellent, Jacob," said Miss Darling as soon as he finished. She was very impressed that Jacob was able to say all of the words to the Pledge perfectly. She had taught hundreds of kindergartners over the past twenty years, and Jacob was one of the only students she had ever taught who knew the Pledge perfectly on the first day of class. He truly was a brilliant kid.

Miss Darling then told her students to sit back down in their seats and explained, "Don't worry, class. By the end of this month, all of you will also know the words to the Pledge of Allegiance. We practice saying it every day in the morning before we start class. The Pledge is a way for us to promise that we will be loyal to our country, which means that we are promising to follow all of the rules. Kids just like you have been saying the Pledge in our country since it was written in 1882, more than 200 years ago."

Jacob raised his hand again.

So, Miss Darling called on him, "Yes, Jacob. Do you have a question?"

"Actually," replied Jacob, "the Pledge of Allegiance was written in 1892."

Miss Darling was surprised. She thought the Pledge was from 1882—not 1892. Miss Darling wondered to herself, *Could I be wrong?* So, she then asked Jacob, "How do you know when the Pledge was written?"

"Because," Jacob answered, "Christopher Columbus led his three ships—the Nina, the Pinta, and the Santa Maria—from Spain in 1492. And Francis Bellamy wrote the Pledge of Allegiance 400 years later in 1892."

Miss Darling was shocked. She couldn't believe it. Jacob sounded smarter than most people, even in high school. "WOW!" she exclaimed. "How do you know all that?" she asked Jacob.

"My sister, Ashley, told me and my parents last year at dinner," answered Jacob. "She had to learn it for a test on U.S. history."

"And you remembered that from more than a year ago?" asked Miss Darling.

"Yeah," replied Jacob. "My parents say that I have an excellent memory."

"You must have an incredible memory," agreed Miss Darling. "That's really going to help you be a terrific student." Miss Darling knew that most young kids aren't able to remember things from so long ago. She realized right then that Jacob was an exceptionally bright young boy.

Jacob smiled after Miss Darling's comments. He was happy that Miss Darling thought he was so smart. But Jacob also was a little embarrassed because all of the other kids were kind of staring at him. It made him feel a little bit uncomfortable—like he wasn't normal. Jacob wanted the other kids to like him, but they were all looking at him like he was a strange alien from another planet. However, the students weren't staring because they thought that Jacob was weird—they actually were staring because they were so impressed and amazed at how smart he was.

After the Pledge of Allegiance discussion, Miss Darling tried to get the class back on track. "Why don't we all now return to today's lesson plan?" she suggested. "We have a lot of work to do this morning, and I want to make sure that we finish before your first recess time."

Right after Miss Darling finished talking, all of the lights in the room suddenly turned off at the same time. The room was completely dark, except for a little bit of sunlight coming through the windows. Then an extremely loud alarm started beeping. It was much louder than the usual tardy bell. Miss Darling looked a little worried as she explained, "Okay, everyone, please pay attention. That's the fire alarm. Everybody, remain calm and listen to my instructions. I need all of you to line up in a single file line by the door, and I will lead you to our safe spot in front of the school."

All the kids did exactly what Miss Darling instructed them to do. They got out of their seats and lined up by the front door. Miss Darling led them out to the front of the school and stopped at a spot right by the flag pole by the school parking lot. Each classroom was going to a different assigned area in front of the school. Jacob could see Ashley waiting with her class by the water fountain, and Prince was with his class by the front gate.

Everybody just waited outside patiently until the principal came out a few minutes later. The principal's name was Principal Crabtree.

"Attention, everyone!" announced Principal Crabtree. Her voice was very loud because she talked through a machine called a megaphone, which sounded like someone turned up the volume on a TV way too high.

Everybody quieted down to listen to the principal after she started speaking.

"Please remain calm," Principal Crabtree instructed. "There is no fire, and there is no immediate danger. You don't have anything to worry about. But we do seem to be having a problem with our lights and electricity. That means we're going to have to shut down the school for the rest of today."

All of a sudden, a bunch of the older kids started screaming, "YAY! NO SCHOOL! YAY!"

Principal Crabtree then yelled, "EVERYBODY, QUIET DOWN!" She sounded especially loud because she was shouting into her megaphone. Once everybody got quiet again, she continued, "Our office is currently calling all of your parents, and they should be here soon to pick you up and take you home. Even if you normally walk to and from school, you still have to wait. Nobody is allowed to walk home without their parents. Please be patient and wait with your teachers."

Waiting for all the parents to show up seemed to take a very long time. Slowly but surely, cars eventually started arriving at the front of the school, and kids got into their parents' cars one by one. Jacob, Ashley, and Prince each waited patiently in their different assigned areas with their teachers.

Finally, Mrs. Pea drove up to the front of the school. Ashley and Jacob both jumped into her car. But Mrs. Pea didn't drive off right away. She rolled down her window and said to Principal Crabtree, "Hi, I'm also here to pick up Prince Gold. His father already spoke with the school office and gave his permission."

"No problem. I understand," replied Principal Crabtree. "Please wait right here, and I'll go get him." Principal Crabtree already knew that Mrs. Pea was allowed to pick up Prince from school. Since Dr. Gold had to work so much, he had signed a permission slip that allowed Mr. and Mrs. Pea to pick Prince up from school and drive him home.

A few minutes later, Principal Crabtree returned to Mrs. Pea's car with Prince by her side. Ashley slid into the middle seat next to Jacob. Prince then opened the car door and sat down right next to Ashley.

"Thank you for getting Prince," Mrs. Pea said to Principal Crabtree. "By the way," she asked, "why exactly did you have to close school early today? What's wrong?"

"It's some sort of lighting problem," responded Principal Crabtree. "I just hope we can get it fixed quickly. We want to get our kids back in school as soon as possible. We don't want them to fall too far behind on their studies."

"What kind of lighting problem?" asked Mrs. Pea. She was very curious. Mrs. Pea thought that it had to be a serious problem if it meant that school had to be closed because of it.

"Well," replied Principal Crabtree, "we don't really know what caused the lights to stop working. It's truly a mystery. Nobody can figure it out. The lights just don't seem to be working, and nobody can figure out why. Somehow, all of the lights in the school just suddenly turned off. We can't seem to get them back on. That's why we had to close the school. We can't have kids going to school without lights—they can't go to school in the dark."

"That does sound like an enormous problem," admitted Mrs. Pea. "It seems like quite a mystery. Good luck fixing the lights."

"Thank you," replied Principal Crabtree. "Have a good day," she added.

"You too," responded Mrs. Pea.

After Principal Crabtree and Mrs. Pea said goodbye to each other, Mrs. Pea started the car and left the school. Jacob, Ashley, and Prince were all sitting quietly in the backseat with enormous smiles on their faces. They were so excited that they got to leave school early.

"Do I still get to go over to Prince's house with Ashley today?" Jacob asked his mom.

"Yes, you do," answered Mrs. Pea. "In fact, Dr. Gold said I could drive you over there right now since school ended so early."

"YAY!" everyone shouted from the backseat.

"Ashley and Jacob," reminded Mrs. Pea, "remember to be on your best behavior at the Gold house."

"Okay," Ashley and Jacob both replied at the same time.

It was a very short drive from the school, past the Pea house, and all the way up the long, curvy driveway to the Gold mansion. Mrs. Pea stopped the car in front of the giant staircase leading up to the front doors of the Gold mansion. As soon as she parked, Jacob, Ashley, and Prince all jumped out.

"Bye, Mom!" yelled Ashley.

"See you later!" shouted Jacob.

"Goodbye, Mrs. Pea," said Prince very politely. "Thanks for the ride," he added. Prince had wonderful manners, and he always tried to remember to say please and thank you.

"Bye, kids," replied Mrs. Pea. "Have fun!"

CHAPTER 6

JACOB'S SPECIAL POWER

Jacob, Ashley, and Prince ran up the stairs to the Gold house. Prince used his key to open the front door, and then Ashley and Jacob followed him into the house.

Dr. Gold heard the door open and yelled, "Is that you, Prince?"

"Yeah, Dad!" Prince shouted back. "Ashley and Jacob are both with me."

"Great!" replied Dr. Gold. "Why don't you all come join me in the kitchen? I have a lot planned for us today."

Jacob followed Prince and Ashley into the kitchen. Since Jacob had never been to the Gold mansion, he didn't know where the kitchen was. As he walked and looked around, Jacob just couldn't believe how large the house was—it was the biggest mansion he'd ever seen. Ashley had told him that Prince had a huge place, but Jacob could never have imagined that anything could be as enormous as this. He wondered if the Gold mansion was even larger than his new elementary school.

Ashley didn't really pay any attention to how big the Gold mansion was. She was used to it since she had been over to Prince's house so many times. Usually, when Ashley came over, she just hung out with Prince either in the kitchen, Prince's room, or the humongous backyard. There were almost twenty other rooms in the house that Ashley had never even seen. Most of those other rooms were empty since Prince and Dr. Gold never used them.

Prince knew that his house was much larger than most people's homes. He thought that he might live in one of the biggest houses in the world. But Prince didn't care that his house was so gigantic. In fact, Prince kind of wished that he lived in a more normal-sized house. He didn't like being so different from all the other kids.

Prince once asked his dad why only the two of them lived in such an enormous home, especially since they didn't even use most of the rooms. Dr. Gold had explained that Prince's mom originally wanted to have a giant house with a ton of rooms so that they could adopt orphans to come to live with them. Orphans are children whose parents have died, and they have no other relatives who can take care of them. Prince's mom wanted to help those kids by giving them a beautiful home and including them as part of her own loving family. But, since Prince's mom was gone, Dr. Gold decided that it would be best if he didn't adopt any kids. Dr. Gold didn't think he would have the time or energy to take care of any adopted kids all by himself, especially without Prince's mom around to help. That's why only Prince and his dad ended up living in such a humongous home by themselves.

"Hello, kids," Dr. Gold said as Jacob, Ashley, and Prince entered the kitchen.

"Hi, Dad," replied Prince.

"Hi, Dr. Gold," said Ashley.

Jacob didn't say anything. Just like on his first day of school that morning, he was shy around new people.

"You must be Jacob," said Dr. Gold in a very friendly voice. "Right?"

Jacob didn't respond with words and only nodded his head a tiny bit up and down. He then looked over at Ashley and shrugged his shoulders. Jacob was acting shy since he didn't feel comfortable talking around new people.

Ashley could tell that Jacob was too shy to talk, so she answered Dr. Gold for him, "Yes, this is my brother, Jacob. He's the one who might have a special power."

Jacob didn't know what Ashley was talking about. He didn't realize that he might have a unique power. Jacob finally spoke out loud, "What special power? What are you talking about?"

"Well," Dr. Gold replied to Jacob, "that's what we're going to try to find out today."

Jacob was really confused. Nobody had ever told him that he might have any kind of extraordinary power. Jacob loved superheroes. He wondered if he might have super strength. Or, even better, what if he could fly?

"Am I a superhero?" Jacob asked Dr. Gold.

Dr. Gold laughed at the thought of Jacob as a superhero. "No," he answered, "I'm sorry to tell you that you are not a superhero. But you might have a special skill that nobody else has. We're going to try to find out how it works."

"What's a skill?" asked Jacob.

Prince tried to explain, "A skill is like a special ability, talent, or power."

Jacob was still confused. He didn't know what ability he had that was so special.

Ashley attempted to describe it to Jacob as well, "You know how you have an excellent memory."

"Yeah," Jacob replied. He knew exactly what Ashley meant. Jacob remembered everything. Even his new kindergarten teacher, Miss Darling, thought he had an amazing memory.

"Well," said Ashley, "that's one of your special skills."

Jacob thought for a second, and then he asked Dr. Gold, "Is my memory my special power?"

"A good memory is certainly very unique," Dr. Gold answered. "But Prince and Ashley seem to think that you have an even more special power that nobody else has."

Jacob was getting frustrated. If his memory wasn't his special power, then what was it? Jacob couldn't think of anything. He knew all about superheroes, and he was pretty sure that he couldn't do any of the super things that superheroes could do. Jacob didn't have super strength; he couldn't fly; he couldn't shoot webs, water, or fire out of his hands; and he couldn't breathe underwater. "So, what's my special power?" he asked Dr. Gold.

"That's what we're all here to find out," replied Dr. Gold. "But first, we need to do some scientific experiments."

Jacob was a little scared because he didn't really know what a scientific experiment was. Jacob remembered seeing a TV show once where the doctors did experiments by putting big needles into people's arms, and he was afraid that Dr. Gold would do that to him.

Jacob absolutely did not want any shots or blood, so he asked Dr. Gold with a worried voice, "Are you going to give me a shot or make me have blood?"

"No, no, no," Dr. Gold quickly replied, trying to calm Jacob down. He could tell that Jacob was concerned by the look on his face. Dr. Gold explained, "I'm sorry, I didn't mean to worry you. We aren't going to do anything like that. There will be absolutely no shots and no blood. Nobody will even touch you. The type of science experiments that we are going to do will only involve a deck of cards and me asking you some questions."

Jacob felt a lot better. Because of Dr. Gold's explanation, he was no longer scared about the science experiments. And he loved to play card games. It sounded like Dr. Gold simply wanted to play card games with him.

Dr. Gold explained further, "With a deck of cards, every card looks the same on the back, but on the front of each card there is either a number—two through ten—or a jack, queen, king, or ace." He then asked, "Do you know what the jack, queen, king, and ace cards look like?"

"Yeah," answered Jacob, "I have a deck of cards at home. Sometimes I get to play card games with Ashley and my parents." Jacob was proud of himself for already knowing all the cards. Jacob added, "I also know that the fronts of all the cards have either red diamonds, red hearts, black clubs, or black spades."

"Perfect!" exclaimed Dr. Gold. "Then it sounds like we are ready to start the science experiment card game."

Jacob was now excited to do the science experiment, especially because he liked card games so much.

Dr. Gold put the deck of the cards in one pile on the table so you couldn't see the front of any of the cards. He then quickly flipped over the first ten cards to show Jacob: (1) a three of clubs; (2) a queen of hearts; (3) a ten of diamonds; (4) a six of clubs; (5) a two of hearts; (6) a nine of diamonds; (7) a five of spades; (8) a jack of hearts; (9) a ten of spades; and (10) a king of clubs. Dr. Gold let Jacob look at the cards for five seconds, and then Dr. Gold flipped the ten cards back over so that Jacob couldn't see the fronts of the cards any longer.

"I don't get it," questioned Jacob. "I don't understand how to play this card game." Jacob was confused, so he then asked, "What are the rules?"

Dr. Gold just laughed. "Of course, you don't get it. I haven't explained the rules to you yet." Dr. Gold then asked Jacob, "Do you remember the ten cards that I showed you?"

Jacob thought it was a very dumb card game. He remembered the ten cards, so he told Dr. Gold, "Yeah, there was a three of clubs, a queen of hearts, a ten of diamonds, a six of clubs, a two of hearts, a nine of diamonds, a five of spades, a jack of hearts, a ten of spades, and a king of clubs."

Prince and Ashley couldn't believe it. How did Jacob remember all of the ten cards? They could only remember a few of the cards.

"Wow!" exclaimed Dr. Gold. "That's extremely impressive." He turned the ten cards back over to check and make sure that Jacob was correct. Dr.

Gold then said, "Most super smart people can only remember three or four cards. You just named every single one of the ten cards perfectly in the correct order."

Ashley asked, "Is that Jacob's special power?"

Dr. Gold answered, "Having an amazing memory is very special, but it's not really a super special power." Some lucky people have what is called a 'photographic memory.' Jacob can remember everything that he sees, just like he is looking at a photograph. His memory also works for things that he might have heard in the past. Even if something happened a really long time ago, Jacob remembers it as if it is right in front of him. It's like he is watching a recording of a TV show in his brain. To Jacob, anything that he sees or hears, he can remember like it only happened one second ago—even if he really saw or heard it years ago."

Prince then asked, "But how was Jacob able to remember seeing the Mystery Man at the airport when he wasn't actually even there?"

"Aha!" replied Dr. Gold. "That's the real question we have to find out today because that really might be a super special power. And in order to find out the answer, we now need to do some more science experiments with the cards."

Jacob was thrilled. He thought he was extremely good at Dr. Gold's card games, and he wanted to play some more as part of Dr. Gold's science experiments.

Dr. Gold then shuffled all the cards. He picked the first card off the top of the deck, looked at the card without showing Jacob, let Prince and Ashley see the card, and then placed the card back in the middle of the deck so that Jacob couldn't see what card it was. Dr. Gold then asked Jacob, "Can you tell me what my card was?"

Jacob answered right away, "It was a seven of clubs." He didn't even have to think about it. Jacob was very proud of himself because he knew he had the correct answer. He could see the card in his head as soon as Dr. Gold looked at it.

Prince and Ashley just stared silently at Dr. Gold with shocked faces. They could not believe that Jacob had named the correct card without actually seeing the card.

"That's right!" replied Dr. Gold with an excited voice. "Hmmm," he said to himself. He thought quietly for a little while, and then he said, "Let's try another one. But this time, I want you to cover your eyes."

"Okay," responded Jacob. He put his hands over his eyes and waited for Dr. Gold to ask him another question.

Dr. Gold then told Prince, "It's your turn to try, Prince. Pick a card from the deck, look at the card without showing Jacob, and then put it back in the middle of the deck."

Prince did exactly what his dad told him to do. He picked a card, looked at it, showed it to only Dr. Gold and Ashley, and then he put the card back in the deck without showing Jacob. Jacob kept his hands covering his eyes the entire time.

"Okay, Jacob," said Dr. Gold, "you can take your hands off of your eyes now." As soon as Jacob removed his hands, Dr. Gold asked, "Can you tell me what Prince's card was?"

"That's easy," replied Jacob. "He had a queen of diamonds." Once again, Jacob was positive he had the correct answer. He could see the card in his head that Prince had picked.

"Jacob is right!" declared Prince excitedly. "That's amazing. How did he do that? Was that a magic trick?" Prince could not believe it. How could Jacob know what the card was without actually looking at the card? There is no way that

Jacob could have cheated because his eyes were covered the entire time.

Dr. Gold chuckled a little and then replied, "No, that definitely was not a magic trick. I can't explain it just yet. I have one more science experiment that we need to do, and then I will know for sure."

Jacob had a huge smile on his face. He thought that he was doing an outstanding job at Dr. Gold's science experiment card games. He also was so happy that he was getting to play with Prince and Ashley at the Gold house.

Dr. Gold then instructed Ashley, "I want you to take another card off the top of the deck. But this time, I don't want anyone to look at the front of the card—not even you, Ashley. Just move the card off the deck and then put it face down next to the deck."

Ashley did exactly as she was told. She took the card off the top of the deck, and then she immediately placed it next to the deck without turning the card over. Nobody had a chance to see what was on the front of the card.

Dr. Gold then asked Jacob, "Can you tell me what Ashley's card was?"

Jacob closed his eyes and concentrated his mind with all his might. After a brief pause, he finally responded with a very sad voice, "No, I don't know what Ashley's card was. I couldn't see it." Jacob was confused and disappointed. He thought that since he didn't know what the card was, it meant that he didn't really have a super special power. Jacob was afraid that he had failed Dr. Gold's experiment. He was about to cry because he thought he was now losing the card game and that nobody would want to play with him anymore. No matter how hard he tried, Jacob just couldn't see Ashley's card in his head.

"Wonderful!" exclaimed Dr. Gold. "I figured it out," he said with joy. Dr. Gold had a smile on his face. He had discovered how Jacob's extraordinary power worked. Jacob could see things through other people's eyes. Dr. Gold thought it was incredible. He had never before read or heard anything about an ability as unique as Jacob's.

"I don't understand," said Jacob to Dr. Gold. "Why is it wonderful?" he asked. Jacob didn't think it was good at all. Because he didn't know what Ashley's card was, he felt he had failed the science experiment and lost the card game. "How is it great that I couldn't see Ashley's card?"

Dr. Gold explained to Jacob, "Actually, you couldn't see any of the cards."

"Huh?" questioned Jacob. Now he was extremely confused, so he said to Dr. Gold, "But I only couldn't see Ashley's card. I did see your card and Prince's card. What do you mean that I couldn't see any of the cards? I did see the first two cards."

"Nope," replied Dr. Gold. "You didn't actually see my card or Prince's card."

"I don't understand either," admitted Prince. "How did he know what the first two cards were, but he didn't know what the last card was?"

"Yeah," agreed Ashley. "That makes no sense. If he didn't see the first two cards, then how did he know which cards they were?"

Dr. Gold finally explained to everybody, "Well, Jacob didn't really see the first two cards with his own eyes. He saw those first two cards through my eyes and through Prince's eyes. He couldn't see Ashley's card because Ashley never turned the card over to see it with her own eyes."

"I still don't understand," complained Jacob. He felt Dr. Gold's explanation wasn't very good. Jacob thought everybody could do what he did. How come only he could see something through somebody else's eyes?

Ashley didn't understand either. She looked just as confused as Jacob.

But Prince wasn't confused anymore. "I think I understand," he said. "I get it now. It makes total sense."

Ashley and Jacob both looked over at Prince for help. They thought he might be able to describe it better than Dr. Gold.

"Let me try to explain," offered Prince. "Jacob can see things in his head that other people are using their eyes to see. Jacob isn't using his own eyes. He is able to use other people's eyes."

Ashley finally understood. "That explains why Jacob couldn't see the last card. Since I never used my own eyes to see it, then he couldn't see it."

"That's right," agreed Dr. Gold. "I used my eyes to see the first card, and Prince used his eyes to see the second card. That's why Jacob could see those two cards, even though he wasn't using his own eyes."

"I think I understand now," said Jacob. He finally understood how his special power worked. "I'm not really seeing things with my eyes. When I see things in my head, it means I'm seeing things through somebody else's eyes."

"Exactly!" exclaimed Dr. Gold.

"Well, is that my special power?" Jacob asked, sounding like he was almost upset.

"Of course, you silly goose," replied Ashley. "Don't you think that's a pretty cool power?"

"No," answered Jacob, "not really." Jacob was very disappointed. He wanted to have an awesome superhero power. Seeing things through somebody else's eyes didn't seem like a true superhero power. Jacob wanted to have an incredible power like super strength or the ability to fly.

"But your power is cool," said Prince. "Nobody else can do what you do."

"Really?" replied Jacob with surprise. He didn't realize that nobody else could see things through other people's eyes. Jacob thought everybody could do that. "Well, what I am supposed to use my special power for?" he asked.

Prince answered, "You could use your special power to win at card games. But," he added, "it wouldn't really be fair if you're able to see everyone else's cards using your special power."

"Wait a minute," said Ashley angrily as she thought to herself. "That explains why Jacob always wins when our family plays card games. Jacob was actually cheating. I don't ever want to play another card game with him again." Ashley was bitter. She used to think that Jacob was simply lucky at card games. She now realized that all this time, Jacob really won because he had been able to see everybody else's cards with his unique power.

Dr. Gold responded, "Calm down, Ashley. You have to understand that Jacob never knew that he had a special power. When he sees something in his head, it looks just the same as if he saw it using his own eyes. Jacob didn't realize that he was using his special power when he played cards with all of you. It can't be cheating if he didn't even know he was cheating."

"I guess you're right," agreed Ashley with a huff. "But I'm still not going to play any more card games with Jacob. No wonder he always wins."

"If I can't use my special power to win card games," said Jacob, "then what should I use my special power for?"

Dr. Gold replied, "There are more important things than card games. I think it would be much more valuable for you to use your special power to help solve crimes. You could be a detective and help stop bad guys from doing bad crimes."

"A detective?" responded Jacob as he thought to himself about the possibility. "That does sound kind of cool," he admitted. Jacob began to get very excited. He was grinning from ear to ear. Jacob was going to get to stop bad guys. He was going to be a detective. Even though he really wanted to be like a superhero, he felt being a detective was also pretty awesome.

"Not so fast, though," said Dr. Gold. He then informed Jacob, "You're going to first have to practice using your special power before you will be ready to help solve crimes as a detective. You need to learn how to use your special power perfectly."

"Okay," sighed Jacob. He actually wanted to be a detective right away, but he knew better than to argue with Dr. Gold. He understood that he had to listen to Dr. Gold and practice using his power, or else Dr. Gold would never let him help solve crimes.

"Don't worry," Prince said to Jacob. "Ashley and I will help you practice. We both have our own special powers too."

"Really?" asked Jacob. He was very surprised since he never knew that Prince and Ashley also had special powers.

"Yes, it's true," replied Ashley. "I can see things that have already happened."

Prince added, "And I can make things move slowly while I move extremely fast. That's how I was able to protect your friend, Luke, from the three bullies on the first day of school."

"This is so cool," exclaimed Jacob. "We all have special powers. We're all special."

Prince then said, "And now you can be in The Super Secret Special Powers Club with Ashley and me."

This was the best day of Jacob's life—it was even better than his birthday. Jacob had a super special power, just like Prince and Ashley. And now he was going to be in The Super Secret Special Powers Club with them. Jacob had never been happier.

CHAPTER 7

START OF WINTER VACATION

The lights at the elementary school were only broken for the first day of school. Nobody could ever figure out why the lights suddenly stopped working, but the lights somehow miraculously started working again on the second day of school. Since there were no more electricity problems at the school, all the students had to go back to school like normal.

For the next few months, Jacob, Ashley, and Prince walked to and from school together every school day. Every Monday, Wednesday, and Friday, they would all go to Prince's house after school to do their homework and practice their super special powers with Dr. Gold. Ashley and Jacob wished they could go to Prince's house every day after school, but Ashley and Jacob had piano lessons on Tuesdays, and Prince had violin lessons on Thursdays.

After the last day of school in December before the start of winter vacation, Jacob, Ashley, and Prince were walking home together with big smiles on their faces. They were all excited about their big winter break—three weeks of vacation with no school and no homework. Most of the houses they walked past had Christmas lights all over them, which looked really cool at night. Some homes even had giant blow-up Santas and Rudolphs, and one house even had a humongous blow-up Grinch on the roof.

"I can't wait for Christmas," said Jacob as they walked by all the houses with Christmas decorations. Even though the homes weren't all lit up because it wasn't dark out yet, the decorations reminded Jacob that he would be getting a ton of presents very soon.

"Me too," Ashley agreed. Ashley and Jacob would argue a lot, but the one thing they totally agreed on was that Christmas was a wonderful holiday.

Prince sighed and then said, "Well, at least I get to celebrate Hanukkah."

Jacob was a little confused by Prince's statement. He didn't really know what Prince was talking about, so he asked, "What is Ha-lay-lu-yaka?"

Prince and Ashley both laughed at how Jacob mispronounced the word.

"What's so funny?" asked Jacob. He didn't realize that he had said anything wrong because he had never actually heard about the holiday called Hanukkah.

"It's pronounced Ha – New – Ka," answered Ashley, saying the word very slowly and clearly.

"Oh," said Jacob as he shrugged his shoulders. He still didn't know what Prince and Ashley were talking about. So, he asked, "What's that?"

Prince replied, "Hanukkah is a holiday that Jewish people celebrate around the same time as Christmas. There are eight days of Hanukkah, and every night you light candles and get a present. The holiday celebrates a battle that happened a long, long time ago where the Jewish people only had enough oil left to have candlelight for one night, but thanks to a miracle from God, the light actually lasted for eight days."

"But then what do you do for Christmas?" asked Jacob. He thought that lighting candles didn't sound nearly as much fun as decorating a Christmas tree, making gingerbread houses, listening to Christmas music, and eating lots of goodies. Although, Jacob did think that getting a new present every night for eight nights sounded pretty cool.

"Well," responded Prince, "a lot of Jewish people don't really celebrate Christmas."

Jacob couldn't believe it. He was shocked. Why would anyone not celebrate Christmas? That was the best holiday of the year. Jacob asked Prince, "Don't you miss all the fun?"

"Yeah," admitted Prince, "I do miss it a little. I mean, we still have some fun on Hanukkah. We get to play Hanukkah games where we spin a toy called a dreidel. We get eight presents. We get to eat coins made out of chocolate. We also get to eat special yummy fried potato pancakes—called latkes—with apple sauce and sour cream."

"That sounds disgusting," replied Ashley as she thought about the food that Prince had described. "You put sour cream and apple sauce on pancakes… Yuck!" Ashley knew that maple syrup and butter tasted good on pancakes. But she had never heard about anyone putting sour cream and apple sauce on them.

Prince laughed out loud. "No, silly. Latkes are not like normal pancakes. They're a special kind of delicious Jewish fried potato food—some people call them potato pancakes only because they're flat and round like pancakes. My dad makes some of the best."

"So, what do you do on actual Christmas?" Ashley asked.

"Well," replied Prince, "usually my dad and I just order Chinese food and hang out at the house watching movies."

Jacob couldn't believe what he just heard. Prince's explanation sounded like the worst Christmas celebration ever. He then suggested, "You should come celebrate with us on Christmas."

Ashley agreed with Jacob, "Yeah, that would be so much fun."

Prince was excited about the thought of joining Ashley and Jacob for Christmas. "Are you sure it would be okay with your parents?" he asked.

"Let's go ask them right now," replied Ashley. The timing was perfect because they had just walked all the way back to Ashley and Jacob's house from school.

Jacob, Ashley, and Prince ran up to the front door, but Mrs. Pea opened the door for them before they even got there. Mrs. Pea had seen them arrive through the window in the Pea house, so she was ready to let them in before they even made it to the door.

"Congratulations, kids," said Mrs. Pea while she held the front door open. "It's finally winter vacation. Are you excited?"

Jacob didn't bother answering Mrs. Pea's question. Before the kids even entered the house, he quickly blurted out, "Can Prince come to our house for Christmas?"

"Please, Mom! Please!" added Ashley in a begging voice.

Mrs. Pea was not expecting such a question and wasn't ready to answer right away. She thought about it for a second and then said, "I guess it's okay with me, but we need to get permission from Prince's dad, Dr. Gold, first."

Just then, Dr. Gold happened to drive by the Pea house. He parked his car in front of the house, opened his window, and shouted out, "Hey, Prince, do you want a ride home?"

Mrs. Pea waved hello to Dr. Gold, and then she stepped outside the house, closed the front door behind her, and walked up to his car to talk to him.

"Why, it's great to see you, Mrs. Pea," said Dr. Gold in a cheerful voice as Mrs. Pea approached the car.

"Thank you. It's always a pleasure to see you as well," replied Mrs. Gold. "Meanwhile, I actually have a question for you," she added.

"Sure, go ahead," said Dr. Gold. "What's your question?"

"Well," replied Mrs. Pea, "the kids and I were wondering if maybe you and Prince might want to join us for a Christmas dinner celebration. I know you're Jewish, so I wasn't sure if it was allowed."

"Of course," said Dr. Gold with glee. He was so happy to be invited to a Christmas dinner. Even though he was Jewish, it did not mean that he wasn't allowed to celebrate non-Jewish holidays with other people. So, he said to Mrs. Pea, "We would be delighted to join you. While we don't celebrate Christmas at our house, we absolutely would love to celebrate the holiday with you at your home. Thank you so much for the invitation."

"Perfect!" exclaimed Mrs. Pea. "Why don't you plan to come over around six on Christmas evening?"

"We wouldn't miss it for the world," responded Dr. Gold.

Mrs. Pea then turned around from the car and told Jacob, Ashley, and Prince, "It's settled. Dr. Gold and Prince will be joining us for Christmas dinner."

Jacob, Ashley, and Prince all ran up to the car when they heard the good news.

"Really?" asked Prince.

Dr. Gold replied, "Yep, we now officially have Christmas plans with the Pea family."

"I can't wait!" said Prince with excitement. "I love Christmas," he added.

Jacob was surprised by Prince's statement. He didn't realize that Jewish people could love Christmas even though it wasn't a Jewish holiday. So, Jacob said to Prince, "But I thought Jewish people don't celebrate Christmas. How can you love it if you don't celebrate Christmas?"

"Well," replied Prince, "just because some Jewish people don't celebrate Christmas at their house doesn't mean that Jewish people don't like

Christmas. Actually, some Jewish people like Christmas so much that they wrote a bunch of the most famous Christmas songs out there."

"Really?" questioned Ashley. She didn't believe Prince and thought he might be joking with her. "Are you being serious?" she asked.

"It's true," responded Dr. Gold. "Have you heard songs like 'Rudolph the Red-Nosed Reindeer,' 'Chestnuts Roasting on an Open Fire,' 'Let It Snow,' 'Santa Baby,' 'It's the Most Wonderful Time of the Year,' 'Silver Bells,' 'Rockin' Around the Christmas Tree,' 'Walking in a Winter Wonderland,' 'A Holly Jolly Christmas,' and 'White Christmas?'"

"Of course," replied Ashley, "I've heard of all those songs." Ashley thought that Dr. Gold was just randomly naming all of the most famous Christmas songs.

"Believe it or not," said Dr. Gold, "Jewish people wrote all of those Christmas songs."

"No way," responded Jacob, who was completely surprised.

"Yes way," replied Prince.

"Wow!" exclaimed Ashley. She couldn't believe it. Ashley realized that Jewish people also could have a ton of Christmas spirit. Since Christmas was her favorite holiday, she was so happy to learn that her best friend Prince also loved the holiday.

Dr. Gold then looked at his watch and said to Prince, "I hate to break up this conversation, but would you like a ride back to our house? We still need to finish setting up all of our Hanukkah decorations."

"Okay, Dad," answered Prince. He jumped in the car, put on his seat belt, and Dr. Gold started driving away.

"Bye, everyone," said Dr. Gold out the open car window as he started to drive away. "Thanks again for the Christmas invitation."

Jacob, Ashley, and Mrs. Pea waved goodbye as Dr. Gold and Prince drove away from the Pea house and up the long, winding driveway to the mansion where they lived.

CHAPTER 8

CHRISTMAS AT THE PEA HOUSE

The following week, on Christmas Day, it was almost time to go to the Pea house for dinner, but Prince wasn't ready yet. He didn't know what he was supposed to wear, and Prince was worried that he would put on the wrong clothes. Dr. Gold and Prince never wore anything special for Hanukkah, so he wasn't sure if he was supposed to dress up for Christmas dinner at the Pea house. Was he allowed to wear shorts or sweatpants? Should he wear jeans? Did he need to wear his brown khakis? Was he supposed to wear a suit and tie?

Dr. Gold shouted out to Prince, "Hurry up and get ready. We need to leave soon." Dr. Gold did not want to be late to the Pea house, and he was excited about Christmas dinner with the Peas.

Prince was nervous, and he did not want to be embarrassed by wearing the wrong clothes. So, he asked his dad, "What am I supposed to wear?"

Dr. Gold quickly responded, "A bathing suit should be good."

"What?" replied a very confused Prince. "Did you say a bathing suit?" he asked. What was his dad talking about? Prince didn't know what to wear, but he thought that a bathing suit had to be the completely wrong thing to wear to a Christmas dinner.

"I'm obviously kidding," said Dr. Gold. "You don't have to be too fancy, but you should look nice. Why don't you wear your khakis, a sweater, and your nice shoes?"

"Oh, okay, fine," replied Prince. He was glad that he now knew what to wear, but he wasn't happy at all. Prince hated wearing his fancy shoes. They were so uncomfortable. Prince couldn't understand why everyone wasn't allowed to wear sneakers all the time, especially since everyone felt they were more comfortable. He once asked his dad why people had to wear uncomfortable fancy shoes, but his dad just told him that it was because they looked nice.

Prince thought that someone should just invent fancy-looking sneakers that are actually comfortable and still look nice. But until that happened, he was stuck wearing his fancy uncomfortable shoes.

Prince threw on his nice clothes and shoes as quickly as possible, and then he ran downstairs to meet his dad. "I'm ready!" he declared.

Dr. Gold looked at Prince for a second and only mumbled, "Hmmm."

Prince could tell that his father noticed a problem, but he didn't know what it was. What could be wrong? He was wearing his brown khaki pants, itchy sweater, and uncomfortable fancy shoes. He was dressed exactly how his dad told him to get dressed. "What's the problem?" asked Prince.

Dr. Gold replied, "Did you forget something?"

Prince couldn't figure out what was missing. He thought to himself, *What could I have forgotten?* He felt like he was fully dressed and ready to go.

Dr. Gold could tell that Prince had no idea what was wrong. Prince felt he was ready to go, but Dr. Gold knew that Prince had forgotten something very important before going out. So, he reminded Prince, "You look very handsome, but don't forget about your hair."

"Oh yeah," sighed Prince as he realized his mistake. He had totally forgotten to brush his hair. It looked all crazy—like it did when he just woke up in the morning. He was supposed to brush his hair for fancy events and even use hair products to keep it from sticking up all over.

Prince ran back upstairs, fixed his hair, and then ran back downstairs in less than five minutes.

"That looks so much better," declared Dr. Gold when he saw Prince. "Now it looks like we're finally ready to go."

Dr. Gold and Prince got into the car, and Dr. Gold then drove them down the long, winding road to the Pea house. Ashley and Jacob opened the front door as soon as they saw the car pull up. They had been patiently waiting by the front door and looking out the window to be ready for their special Christmas dinner guests.

Dr. Gold and Prince got out of their car, walked up to the front of the house, and then followed Ashley and Jacob into the home. Once everyone was inside, both Mr. and Mrs. Pea exclaimed, "Welcome! Merry Christmas!"

Dr. Gold responded, "Thank you! And Merry Christmas to you as well."

Prince added, "Merry Christmas, everyone!"

The Pea house looked like a winter wonderland. There was an enormous Christmas tree in the living room—it was completely covered with ornaments and had a glittery star on top. There also were big stuffed stockings hung over the fireplace mantle. And there were all sorts of Santa Claus, reindeer, and snowmen decorations all over the house.

"Your house looks amazing," mentioned Dr. Gold.

"Thank you," replied Mrs. Pea. "I must admit that we all have a lot of Christmas spirit."

"You haven't even seen the best part yet," added Mr. Pea.

"What's that?" asked Prince.

"Dinner!" answered Mr. Pea with excitement. "Wait until you see the Christmas feast."

Prince couldn't wait. He loved to eat, and he was always hungry. He was so happy that the Pea family invited him and his dad to their Christmas dinner.

Mrs. Pea then asked everyone to sit down at the dining room table. Everything was set up in a very fancy manner—like at an expensive restaurant. There were crystal glasses, bright white porcelain plates, thick cloth napkins, and shiny silverware.

"Before we start eating," instructed Mr. Pea, "I would like to say a little prayer."

Mr. Pea, Mrs. Pea, Jacob, and Ashley then reached out their hands to grab the hand of the person sitting next to them. Dr. Gold and Prince followed their lead so that everyone was holding someone else's hand in a big circle.

Mr. Pea began his prayer, "We are all so grateful to be together today on Christmas. We thank you, God, for our family and friends and for our health. We pray for your blessing, for joy in our hearts, for the ability to forgive, and for peace on earth. May there be food for the hungry, love for all people, healing for the sick, and wisdom for all."

Mrs. Pea chimed in, "Don't forget about the food."

Mr. Pea chuckled and added, "Oh yeah. And thank you, God, for this delicious feast we are about to enjoy. And also thank you to Mrs. Pea for cooking and baking all the delicious food we are about to eat."

Everyone then said together, "Amen," and they all dropped their hands so they could start eating dinner. The food was incredible—it was like a Thanksgiving dinner, but fancier and with more food. The kids even got to drink sparkling apple cider as a special treat.

After dinner—as everyone was finishing up dessert with three different types of pie, vanilla ice cream, and homemade whipped cream—the phone rang at the Pea house.

"I wonder who that could be on Christmas night," said Mr. Pea when he heard the phone ring.

"I'm guessing it might be important," replied Mrs. Pea. "I can't imagine who it is, but I better check."

Mrs. Pea walked over to the house phone in the kitchen and answered it. Everyone quieted down at the dining room table so it wouldn't be too noisy for Mrs. Pea to talk on the phone.

"Hello, this is the Pea residence," said Mrs. Pea as she answered the phone. "Mrs. Chang?… Oh no!… That is horrible news… Yes, of course, I can help… Okay, I will start working on it right away."

Everyone at the table could tell there was a big problem. Mrs. Pea's voice on the phone sounded very concerned.

"Is everything okay, honey?" asked Mr. Pea.

"No, not really," answered Mrs. Pea. "I just got off the phone with Mrs. Chang. She told me that the police arrested her son Johnny and his friend

Marcus. They have been accused of stealing diamonds from the local jewelry store, and they need my help."

Mrs. Pea was a lawyer who helped people. She used to work at a big law firm located on the top floor of the tallest skyscraper in the city. However, after Jacob was born, Mrs. Pea stopped working at the big law firm to spend more time taking care of Ashley and Jacob. Now she worked as a lawyer out of her office at the Pea house to help people with legal problems who could not afford to pay for an expensive attorney. Everyone in the neighborhood knew that Mrs. Pea was one of the best lawyers in town, especially because of all the excellent work that she did to help people. And, apparently, Mrs. Chang really needed Mrs. Pea's help with her son Johnny's legal problems since he and his friend Marcus had been accused of stealing, which is a major crime. Everyone knows that stealing is wrong, and since it is against the law, Johnny and Marcus could have to go to jail if they actually stole the diamonds from the jewelry store.

"Who is Mrs. Chang?" asked Jacob.

Ashley knew who Mrs. Chang was because Mrs. Chang's daughter, Scarlett, was one of her good friends. The two girls had been friends together since preschool. They even took piano lessons from the same teacher and performed at the same recitals every year—including the recent annual holiday concert. Ashley responded to Jacob's question, "Mrs. Chang is my friend Scarlett's mom. Johnny is her older brother in high school."

"Why did Johnny and Marcus steal diamonds?" asked Prince. He thought that seemed like a really bad and dumb thing to do. It was wrong, it was illegal, and it would get you in a ton of trouble—like jail.

"That's what doesn't make sense," replied Mrs. Pea. "According to Mrs. Chang, Johnny and Marcus didn't steal anything. Johnny was playing basketball this afternoon with his friend Marcus at the park. The police came and arrested both Johnny and Marcus because Miss Klanner told the police that she saw Johnny and Marcus steal the diamonds."

"Who is Miss Klanner?" asked Ashley.

"Well," began Mrs. Pea, "Miss Klanner is the elderly woman who owns the local jewelry store, called Klanner Jewels, where the diamonds were stolen."

Mr. Pea then added, "Her whole name is Katherine K. Klanner, and she's also a member of the Ku Klux Klan."

"What's the Koo – Koo – Can?" asked Jacob, pronouncing each word slowly but incorrectly.

Mr. Pea chuckled a little and then corrected Jacob, "It's the Ku – Klux – Klan, not the Koo – Koo – Can. It's also known as the KKK, which is a group of people who want to kick everyone out of this country unless they are Christian with white skin. It's unfortunate, but people like Miss Klanner who are members of the KKK don't like people who have a different skin color or different religion than them."

"That's crazy," said Ashley. "Scarlett Chang is one of my favorite people in the whole world, and she is one of the top students in our class at school. And her older brother, Johnny, is always so nice. Why would Miss Klanner not like them?"

"Well," suggested Mrs. Pea, "Miss Klanner might not like Scarlett and Johnny because their family was originally from Asia. Since Asian people don't have white skin, Miss Klanner doesn't think they belong in our country. And since Marcus has black skin, Miss Klanner probably doesn't like him either."

"What about me?" questioned Prince. "I'm Jewish, and I've never even met Miss Klanner. Why would she not like me?"

"Well," said Mr. Pea, "maybe Miss Klanner never learned that it's important to treat everyone equally regardless of their religion or the color of their skin. Maybe her parents didn't teach her that we are supposed to be nice to everyone—even if they look different or have a different religion. Instead, maybe Miss Klanner's parents taught her to hate instead of to love."

Mrs. Pea then explained, "Right now, we just need to focus on Johnny and his friend Marcus. I'm sure there is a logical and reasonable explanation about what happened to the diamonds at Miss Klanner's jewelry store. And it is now my job to help solve the crime and prove that Johnny and Marcus weren't the bad guys who stole the diamonds. I need to convince the police and the judge that Johnny and Marcus are innocent."

Dr. Gold sat silently at the dining room table. He knew how bad the KKK was, and he thought Miss Klanner might not be telling the truth about Johnny and Marcus stealing diamonds from her store. This certainly was a mystery—and Dr. Gold was thinking to himself that Jacob, Ashley, and Prince might be able to help solve the mystery as detectives using their super secret special powers.

"Well," said Mrs. Pea, "I hate to be a party pooper, but I need to get to work right away to start helping Johnny and Marcus."

"No problem," replied Dr. Gold. "It's getting late anyway, and I'm sure we're all stuffed from your amazing meal."

Prince was still eating his fourth piece of pie for dessert, but he nodded his head in agreement because he could tell that it was time to go home.

"If it would make it easier on you, why don't you send the kids over to my place tomorrow morning so you can work on your legal case?" Dr. Gold suggested to Mrs. Pea.

"That would be great," replied Mrs. Pea. "Thank you," she added.

Dr. Gold wasn't just trying to give Mrs. Pea a break from her two children. He knew that Ashley and Jacob had special powers, and he thought they might be able to use their powers to help solve the mystery of who stole the diamonds from Miss Klanner's jewelry store.

"At least we get to see each other tomorrow," said Prince.

"Can't wait," replied Ashley.

"Yay!" exclaimed Jacob. He was just happy that he would get to play with Prince and Ashley again at Prince's house.

Dr. Gold and Prince then thanked the Pea family for the delicious dinner and drove back home.

After they got back to their house, Dr. Gold and Prince lit some Hanukkah candles and said a special holiday prayer. They then played a dreidel game together until it was Prince's bedtime, at which point Prince put on his pajamas, brushed his teeth, and fell right to sleep.

Unlike Prince, Dr. Gold wasn't able to sleep right away. He stayed up for hours wondering about the jewelry store robbery. He thought to himself, *Why would Miss Klanner say that Johnny and Marcus stole diamonds from her jewelry store? Did Johnny and Marcus really do it, or could there be another explanation?*

CHAPTER 9

MEETING AT THE GOLD HOUSE

The day after Christmas, Ashley and Jacob both woke up very late. They had no school, no homework, and they had stayed up late the night before playing with all of their new Christmas presents. After breakfast, they brushed their teeth and got dressed.

"Are you ready to go to Prince's house?" Ashley asked Jacob.

"Yeah, let's go," said Jacob energetically.

"I think you forgot something," mentioned Ashley.

Jacob had to think for a moment. He looked down at his feet and realized he was only wearing socks. "Whoops," he declared, "I forgot my shoes."

Ashley was used to Jacob forgetting his shoes. Even though Jacob was very smart and had an amazing memory, for some reason, he would forget obvious things like putting on both sneakers. Once Mrs. Pea drove Ashley and Jacob to the supermarket and then realized that Jacob was only wearing one shoe—he had somehow left his other shoe at home. Ashley could not understand how that could happen. How does someone forget to put on both sneakers?

After Jacob had put on and tied his shoes, Ashley and Jacob said goodbye to their parents, and then they walked all the way up the long, winding road to Prince and Dr. Gold's house at the top of the hill.

Once they were there, Jacob ran up the front stairs of the Gold mansion to ring the doorbell. For some reason, Jacob always wanted to be the one to push buttons—like doorbells and on elevators. Ashley used to fight with Jacob about whose turn it was to press the button, but now that she was older and more mature, she just let Jacob do it whenever he wanted. After the doorbell rang, Prince came and opened the enormous, dark, polished wood doors to let Ashley and Jacob in the house.

"Hi, guys!" said Prince.

"Hi," replied Ashley.

"Yo," responded Jacob. Usually, he would have just said 'hi,' but Jacob was trying to act cool in front of Prince and Ashley. He thought saying 'yo,' would sound like a cooler and older big kid. But actually, Prince and Ashley both felt Jacob sounded kind of silly. However, they didn't say anything about it to Jacob since they were being nice and didn't want to hurt Jacob's feelings.

Dr. Gold was talking on the phone when everyone arrived, but he put his phone down for a second after Ashley and Jacob entered the home. "Hello, kids," he said very politely. "I have a bunch of work that I need to do in my basement laboratory, but why don't we have a meeting of The Super Secret Special Powers Club later tonight? I think I'm going to need your detective help to solve the mystery of Miss Klanner's jewelry store robbery."

Dr. Gold had a very important and busy job inventing all kinds of secret science gadgets, so even though he wanted to start solving the mystery of the stolen diamonds, he first had to get all of his other work done.

Before anyone could even respond to Dr. Gold, he grabbed his phone and started talking on it again. Dr. Gold pulled a small key out of his pocket to open the lock on the door going to the basement and then walked down the stairs to his basement laboratory to go to work, closing the door behind him.

"Why don't we go outside and play on the trampoline?" proposed Prince. There were a ton of fun things to do at Prince's house. Not only did Prince have a large trampoline in the backyard, but he also had a tennis court, a basketball court, a swimming pool, and a jacuzzi. Inside the house, he had a video game room with every game you could imagine, a bowling alley, and an ice-skating rink. There was even an enormous movie room with a TV the size of a movie theater and 40 plush, comfy seats.

"I love trampolines," announced Jacob.

"Sounds good to me," agreed Ashley.

Jacob, Ashley, and Prince played most of the day outside, except for a lunch break where Prince ate more than both Ashley and Jacob combined. They also watched a funny Christmas movie on the gigantic TV screen in the movie room, and Prince even made popcorn with extra butter to go with the show.

After the movie, Jacob, Ashley, and Prince had three medium pizzas for dinner. Actually, Ashley and Jacob only shared one of the pizzas, and Prince ate the entire other two pizzas all by himself. Ashley and Jacob could not believe how much Prince ate. Even though Prince was a skinny kid, he had the biggest appetite that anyone had ever seen.

Dr. Gold walked into the kitchen as everyone was finishing their dinner. He had been working in his basement laboratory all day on his secret government science projects, and now he was finally ready to start trying to solve the mystery of the robbery at Miss Klanner's jewelry store.

"Hi, ki…" Dr. Gold started to say. But then, suddenly, all of the lights in the Gold mansion went out. They just turned off. Since it was nighttime, the house was completely dark.

"What's going on?" asked Ashley. "Why did the lights go out?" She was worried because lights aren't supposed to just suddenly turn off. There wasn't any big rain or wind storm, so she couldn't understand why all the electricity would suddenly go out.

"I'm scared," cried Jacob. He did not like the dark. Even at night, he still slept with a nightlight so he wouldn't have bad dreams.

"I don't know what happened," replied Dr. Gold. "There's no storm, so I don't know why the lights would go out. I better go check the electricity box in the garage. Maybe I can figure out the problem there."

Dr. Gold grabbed a flashlight out of one of the drawers in the kitchen. He also pulled out a couple of candles and candlesticks from a different drawer, put them on the kitchen table, and then lit them with a small lighter he had nearby.

As Dr. Gold lit the candles, he said, "You kids better stay here in the kitchen. I don't want you walking around here in the dark because you might bang into something and hurt yourself. These candles will give you a little bit of light."

"WAIT!" shouted Jacob out of nowhere. "What about the Mystery Man?"

"What are you talking about?" asked Dr. Gold. "Why do you want me to wait?" He didn't think Jacob was making any sense. The Mystery Man wasn't with them. Only Jacob, Ashley, Prince, and Dr. Gold were in the kitchen.

"It's the Mystery Man," repeated Jacob. "He was at the airport, and he was also at my dad's bank on the day of the robbery last year. And now he's in your garage. I can see him with my special power."

"How can you be sure it's the Mystery Man?" asked Prince. "Maybe it's somebody else."

Jacob responded, "It's the same Mystery Man. I'm sure. He's wearing the same big black coat, cowboy hat, and sunglasses that he was wearing at the bank and the airport. I can't see his face because his head is kind of hidden by the big cowboy hat and dark sunglasses."

"Uh-oh," responded Dr. Gold. "This is a big problem."

Dr. Gold didn't know what to do, and he was very concerned. He silently thought to himself, *How am I supposed to stop the Mystery Man?*

The Mystery Man could make himself invisible, and Dr. Gold wasn't sure how to catch an invisible person. He didn't want the kids to be scared, but even he was a little frightened. The most important thing, he thought, was to protect the kids from the Mystery Man.

"It will be okay," Dr. Gold assured the kids. "I want you to remain calm and not worry. I'm going to stay here with you and keep you safe."

Even though Dr. Gold told them not to worry, Prince and Ashley were both very concerned and looked very scared. But Jacob didn't appear scared at all. He seemed like he knew that everything was going to be just fine.

Jacob could tell that Prince and Ashley were afraid of the Mystery Man. Ashley was even shaking a little bit because she was so frightened.

"You don't have to worry anymore," said Jacob. "Prince's mom just scared the Mystery Man away, so he can't hurt us."

"JACOB – ALEXANDER – PEA!" yelled Ashley. Whenever she was extremely angry with Jacob, she always called him by his full name. And this time, Ashley was furious. She explained to Jacob, "I already told you before that Prince's mom, Mrs. Gold, died a long time ago. That's not very nice of you to talk about seeing Prince's mom in front of Prince since she's no longer alive. You're going to hurt his feelings."

"But," cried Jacob, "it is his mom. It's Mrs. Gold. It's the same person in the picture over there with Prince and Dr. Gold." Jacob pointed to a framed photo on the kitchen counter—it was a picture of Prince when he was a little toddler standing with his mom and dad. Jacob explained further, "I could see her when I used my special power. I could see Mrs. Gold looking at the Mystery Man, and I could see the Mystery Man looking at Mrs. Gold. I could see it in my head looking through their eyes."

Dr. Gold was in shock. He believed Jacob was telling the truth, but he couldn't understand how Jacob saw his wife because he thought she was dead.

"Let me see if I understand," said Dr. Gold to Jacob. "You saw Mrs. Gold looking at the Mystery Man, and you saw the Mystery Man looking at Mrs. Gold. You were able to see both of them using your special power."

"That's right," answered Jacob.

Prince just sat there silently. He didn't know what to say. His dad had told him many years ago that his mom had died when he was very young, but he never knew exactly how she died. His dad never really explained it to him.

Dr. Gold looked at the photo that Jacob had pointed to. He went over, grabbed the picture, and brought it back to the kitchen table. He then asked Jacob again, "Are you certain that you saw this same woman? Take a very, very close look. Are you absolutely sure?"

"Yes," answered Jacob. "I'm sure. I'm positive. She's the same person. Ashley saw her too at the bank last year after we caught the bank robber, Mr. Wentworth, at my dad's bank."

"Is that true?" Prince asked Ashley. "Did you really see my mom at the bank last year?"

"Well, uh… maybe," answered Ashley, who wasn't really sure. She remembered seeing a beautiful woman at the bank last year with Jacob. It was right after Mr. Pea's boss, Mr. Wentworth, was arrested and sent to jail for robbing the bank. The woman Ashley saw did look a lot like Prince, but then the woman quickly disappeared.

Ashley explained, "I did see a beautiful woman at the bank who kind of looked like you. But I didn't think it could actually be your mom because you had told me that your mom had died."

"What do you think now?" asked Prince. "Look at the picture of her with me and my dad. Do you think the woman you saw at your dad's bank could've been my mom?"

"I guess… maybe," Ashley slowly responded with uncertainty. She then remembered how the woman at the bank had a bag with Prince's photo in it. She explained to Prince, "After the woman disappeared at the bank, she left a paper bag behind—like the kind you get at the grocery store. I looked in the bag and thought I saw a picture of you inside of it. I wondered why the woman left a photo of you inside of the bag, but then when I looked back into the bag a second time to make sure it was your picture, there was nothing there. It was gone. It was like the photo just disappeared. I was afraid that I just imagined seeing your picture and that it was never really there. That's why I never told you about it. I didn't want you to think I was crazy."

Ashley now wondered if maybe it really was Prince's mom, Mrs. Gold. Is it possible that Prince's mom never really died?

Prince was extremely confused. He hadn't seen his mom since he was a very young boy. He believed she was dead because that's what his dad had told him. Had Ashley and Jacob truly seen her? Could she still be alive?

"I didn't think it was possible," said Dr. Gold with tears in his eyes. But these weren't sad tears. Dr. Gold was crying because he was happy—they were happy tears. Dr. Gold had believed his wife,

Prince's mom, was dead. But maybe she wasn't gone. She might still be alive. Dr. Gold never stopped loving his wife, and he had missed her so much. Dr. Gold didn't fully understand what was happening, but he shared, "Maybe it's true. Maybe she's actually back."

"What's going on?" Prince asked his dad. "I don't get it. You said Mom died. How could Ashley and Jacob have seen her?"

"Well," explained Dr. Gold, "I never told you the whole truth. I'm so sorry, and I should never have lied to you. Your mom disappeared when you were very young. Nobody really knew what had happened to her. Somehow her car had driven off the side of a steep mountain cliff and crashed into the ocean below. But nobody was ever able to find her body. Everyone simply assumed that she had died and that her body disappeared in the ocean somewhere. I thought it would be easier to explain to you if I just told you that she died since that is what everybody believed had happened. I didn't know what else to tell you. I didn't want you to think that your mom was alive because I didn't think she could survive such a crash. I was afraid that if you thought she was still alive, then you would be very angry that she left and never came back to see you. Will you please accept my apology? Could you ever forgive me? I'm so sorry."

"Yes, Dad, of course," replied Prince in a sweet and loving manner. He loved his dad, and he knew that his father loved him too. Dr. Gold didn't really lie to Prince because he truly believed Mrs. Gold had died. Dr. Gold was just as surprised and excited as Prince to hear that Mrs. Gold might actually still be alive.

Prince said to his dad, "I know you were just trying to make me feel better. But it sounds like she might be back. I barely even remember her since she left so long ago." Prince had a million questions about his mom and about what had happened to her. He asked, "Why do you think she left? Why do you think she came back? What do you think happened to her? How did she disappear?"

"Those are all good questions," responded Dr. Gold. "Unfortunately, I don't have any answers right now. I'm just as confused as you are."

Suddenly, all of the lights came back on in the Gold mansion. They all turned on exactly at the same time. Dr. Gold turned off his flashlight and blew out the candles on the kitchen table.

"How did all the lights turn back on?" asked Ashley.

"I don't know," answered Dr. Gold. "This is really strange. There are a lot of mysteries—the lights at our house, the Mystery Man, and Mrs. Gold."

Prince added, "And don't forget about the mystery of the robbery at Miss Klanner's jewelry store."

Ashley then chimed in, "Do you think the same Mystery Man also made the lights go out at our school on the first day back after summer vacation?"

"It sounds like we have a ton of mysteries to solve," said Dr. Gold. "And I think all of these mysteries are somehow related to the Mystery Man."

"I can help," announced Jacob proudly. "I have a special power that I can use to be a detective."

"You're absolutely right," agreed Dr. Gold. "We can definitely use your help to solve all of these mysteries. In fact, we are going to need the entire Super Secret Special Powers Club to help. Why don't you tell us what else you were able to see using your special power to see things through other people's eyes?"

Jacob thought for a moment. He closed his eyes and tried to remember all the things that he saw in his head using his special power. Jacob explained, "I saw the Mystery Man holding a small black box with a bunch of buttons on it. It looked a little bit like a toaster oven. He pressed some of the buttons on the machine, and then all the lights went out in this house."

"That's amazing," said Dr. Gold. "What else did you see?"

Jacob continued, "I also saw Mrs. Gold start yelling at the Mystery Man. I couldn't hear what she was saying, but it looked like she was extremely angry. The Mystery Man then pressed some of the buttons on the machine and disappeared. As soon as the Mystery Man was gone, then all the lights came back on."

"What happened to my mom?" asked Prince. He wanted to run up and see her as quickly as possible.

"I don't really know," replied Jacob. "After the Mystery Man disappeared and the lights came back on, Mrs. Gold somehow just disappeared too."

"I can't imagine why she didn't stay," wondered Dr. Gold out loud. "Where has she been all these years, and why did she suddenly return? And how does she know the Mystery Man?"

Jacob, Ashley, and Prince just stared at Dr. Gold. They didn't have any answers to any of Dr. Gold's questions.

"We've also got a big problem with the Mystery Man," declared Dr. Gold. "Based on Jacob's description, it sounds like the Mystery Man has a light control machine just like the one I invented."

"What are you talking about?" asked Prince.

"You know, the light control machine," repeated Dr. Gold. "Remember how the Mystery Man ended up stealing the wrong suitcase at the airport with all of my dirty underwear and socks. I told you that the bag the Mystery Man was really trying to steal had special science equipment that could control all the lights in a building."

"Oh yeah," replied Prince. "I had totally forgotten about that."

Dr. Gold explained, "It sounds like the Mystery Man might have figured out a way to control lights without my special science equipment. He must have created his own similar light control machine."

"Do you think the Mystery Man also turned off all the lights at the school?" asked Ashley.

"That's an excellent question, Ashley," answered Dr. Gold. "I guess it's possible. I wonder if the

Mystery Man who turned off the lights at this house also was able to turn off all the lights at your school. But I can't figure out why the Mystery Man wanted to turn all the lights off at your school and then again at my house. And I need to figure out what happened to Mrs. Gold, and how she was able to stop the Mystery Man. Also, I wonder if somehow any of this has anything to do with the missing diamonds from Miss Klanner's jewelry store."

"How are we going to figure everything out?" asked Prince.

"We're going to have to do some serious detective work," explained Dr. Gold. "But," he added, "we will have to wait until another day. It's getting late, and Ashley and Jacob need to get home."

"He's right," agreed Ashley. "Jacob and I don't want to be late for bedtime. We'll get in trouble if we don't get home before eight at night."

"Do you think we can be detectives tomorrow?" asked Jacob. He loved being part of The Super Secret Special Powers Club with Prince and Ashley, and he wanted to help using his special power.

"I think that's a great idea," replied Dr. Gold. "Since you don't have class tomorrow because of winter vacation, I think we should start by first visiting your school together to do some detective work. Since that is where the lights first went out many months ago, then that's where we should start our investigation. Maybe we can find some clues about the Mystery Man and Mrs. Gold." He then proposed, "Let's all plan to meet at the school at nine tomorrow morning?"

"Okay," replied Ashley. As she got ready to leave, she added, "See you tomorrow morning, Prince. Bye, Dr. Gold."

Jacob was no longer shy around Dr. Gold. He said with his very best manners, "Thank you, Dr. Gold, and thank you, Prince, for letting me come over." Jacob knew that his parents would be very proud of him for remembering his manners.

After Dr. Gold and Prince said goodbye, Ashley and Jacob ran down the long, curvy road back to their little house at the bottom of the hill. They made it just in time so that Mr. and Mrs. Pea wouldn't be angry at them for coming home late.

CHAPTER 10

DETECTIVES AT SCHOOL

Before Dr. Gold and Prince went to the school the following morning, Dr. Gold thought they might need some extra help from his old friend, Agent Putty. Dr. Gold and Agent Putty had been best friends for dozens of years. When they were younger, they both went to the same elementary school, middle school, high school, and college together. After they finished school, Agent Putty joined the FBI, which is the part of the government that helps catch bad guys. The FBI is kind of like a special version of the police. Whenever the local neighborhood police can't solve a crime because it is too big of a mystery, then they ask the FBI to help since FBI agents are some of the very best detectives in the entire world.

Dr. Gold pulled out his cell phone and dialed his friend Agent Putty's number. "Hey, buddy," he said into the phone.

"What's going on?" asked Agent Putty on the phone. He recognized Dr. Gold's voice right away, and he could see that it was Dr. Gold calling him because of caller I.D. on his phone.

"The Super Secret Special Powers Club needs your help," replied Dr. Gold. "I think the Mystery Man is back. You have to come meet me right away so we can try to catch him. We're headed to Prince's school right now."

"No problem," Agent Putty responded. "I know exactly where the school is, and I can be there in ten minutes." Agent Putty already knew about The Super Secret Special Powers Club because he had helped Dr. Gold, Prince, and Ashley solve the mystery of the robbery at Mr. Pea's bank last year. He was aware that Prince and Ashley had special powers because they used their powers to catch Mr. Wentworth—Mr. Pea's old boss and one of the bad bank robbers. Agent Putty did not yet know that Jacob also had special powers and was now part of

The Super Secret Special Powers Club, but he was about to find out.

After they ended their conversation, Dr. Gold and Agent Putty both hung up their phones. Dr. Gold finished getting ready, and then he drove Prince to the school to meet up with Agent Putty. Since they were going right by the Pea house, they picked up Ashley and Jacob on the way.

Dr. Gold and the kids were in the first car to arrive at the school. Since the school was closed, nobody else was there. On a typical day, the parking lot would have been full of cars, and the school would have been swarming with kids. But since it was still winter vacation, the school was completely silent. It was strange to see everything so empty on a weekday. Even though it was Monday, it looked like it was a weekend.

While Dr. Gold and the children were waiting, a big, dark black car raced down the street toward the school. The car pulled right up to the front of the school, where Dr. Gold and the others were standing.

Agent Putty rolled down his car window and said, "I got here as fast as I could." Agent Putty was wearing a dark black suit, a black tie, and dark sunglasses. He wore the same outfit every day to work. Hidden inside his black jacket, he always carried a gun for his job, which he needed to protect people from bad guys. Agent Putty was kind of like a policeman who wears a fancy business suit instead of a police uniform.

"Hi, everyone," said Agent Putty to Dr. Gold and the kids as soon as he got out of the car.

"Hey, buddy," replied Dr. Gold as he went to give his best friend, Agent Putty, a hug.

Even though it had been a long time since Jacob, Ashley, and Prince had seen Dr. Gold's friend, Agent Putty, they still remembered him from when he helped solve the mystery of the robbery at the bank last year.

"Hi," Ashley and Jacob both said back to Agent Putty.

"Mur med me mart?" asked Prince. He had a hard time pronouncing his words because he was still chewing his food. Prince's mouth was stuffed with an enormous bite of a granola bar.

"What did you say?" asked Ashley. She couldn't understand a single word that Prince had just said.

Prince quickly finished chewing and swallowing the rest of his food. "Sorry," he responded, "I meant, where should we start?"

"Oh, that makes more sense," replied Ashley. She then advised Prince, "You really shouldn't talk with food in your mouth. That's terrible manners." Mr. and Mrs. Pea liked to teach Ashley and Jacob all about good manners. And one of the first and most important rules is never talking with your mouth full.

"Yeah, I know," admitted Prince. "But sometimes I just forget."

"Didn't you already eat breakfast before you came here?" asked Jacob. Mrs. Pea always made sure that Ashley and Jacob ate breakfast before leaving the house in the morning. Mrs. Pea would always remind them that breakfast was the most important meal of the day. She liked to say that if you don't start the day with a good breakfast, then you will be cranky and tired for the rest of the day.

"Yes, of course," answered Prince. "I ate breakfast after I woke up. I've already had three bowls of cereal, two waffles, and a muffin. I was still hungry, so I brought four granola bars with me to the school." Prince checked his pockets and then added, "I still have one granola bar left. Do you want it?"

"No, thank you," said Jacob. He couldn't wait to tell his mom about how he remembered to use his best manners. He also couldn't believe how much Prince had eaten for breakfast—Jacob was still full from breakfast after only one big bowl of cereal.

"So," Prince asked again more clearly without any food in his mouth, "where should we start with our detective work?"

Dr. Gold replied, "Let's start our investigation by reviewing all of the clues that we have." He then explained each clue so that everyone would know all the mysteries that they needed to solve:

> Number One: The Mystery Man helped Mr. Wentworth rob a bank last year using a machine that could make him invisible.
>
> Number Two: The Mystery Man was at the airport, and he tried to steal my special science equipment that could control lights.
>
> Number Three: Your school had to close down on the first day because the lights mysteriously stopped working.

Number Four: There was a robbery at Miss Klanner's jewelry store, Klanner Jewels, where diamonds were stolen.

Number Five: Miss Klanner told the police that she saw Johnny and Marcus steal the diamonds, even though the two boys said that they didn't do it.

Number Six: The Mystery Man came to my house and turned off all the lights using a light control machine.

And, last but not least, Number Seven: Even though we all thought she was dead, Mrs. Gold was at the house arguing with the Mystery Man before she and the Mystery Man both disappeared.

"That all sounds about right," Ashley agreed.

"Wow!" exclaimed Prince. "We have so many mysteries to solve. We're going to have to be really good detectives."

Jacob nodded his head in agreement and added, "I can be a good detective with my special power."

Agent Putty considered Dr. Gold's clues and then summarized, "So, it looks like we need to find the Mystery Man, Mrs. Gold, and whoever stole the diamonds from Klanner Jewels."

"That's correct," agreed Dr. Gold.

Prince counted on his fingers and said, "Three."

Ashley was confused by Prince's statement. What was he talking about? Why did he randomly say the number three? So, she asked Prince, "Three what?"

"Oh," replied Prince, "I meant three things." He realized that he didn't fully explain the reason for his number. "We're going to have to be great detectives to find the three things that Agent Putty said: the Mystery Man, my mom, and the diamond thieves."

"Well, then," said Dr. Gold, "I guess it sounds like we're ready to get to work and start our investigation. The first thing we're going to need to do is…"

Before Dr. Gold could say another word, there was a big crashing sound. It came from a storage building across from where they were all standing. Everyone walked across the school parking lot over to the door of the room where the noise came from, which was marked with a sign that said 'Maintenance Only.'

"What's this room for?" asked Jacob. Even though he had just started kindergarten at the school, he had never actually been inside the storage building, and he didn't know what 'Maintenance' meant.

Ashley answered Jacob's question, "This is where the janitor who cleans our school keeps all of his cleaning supplies. Didn't your kindergarten teacher tell you that you weren't allowed to go in there?"

"Oh yeah," replied Jacob. He remembered his teacher, Miss Darling, saying something about the building on the first day of school, but he wasn't really paying attention because he had been talking to his friend Luke.

Dr. Gold tried to open the door to the building, but it was locked.

"Don't worry," said Agent Putty, "I've got this." He then took out a small set of tools from his jacket pocket and inserted a couple of thin metal pieces that looked like tiny pencils into the door lock. Agent Putty slowly moved the metal tools in a circular motion inside the lock until there was a soft clicking sound as the door unlocked.

"Abracadabra!" declared Agent Putty. He was pretending to sound like a magician since he was able to open the locked door. But everyone knew that he really opened it with his special tools—not with magic.

After Agent Putty opened the door, everyone stared inside the room. There was broken glass all over the floor.

Dr. Gold was concerned when he saw the broken glass. How did the glass break on the floor? Dr. Gold, Agent Putty, Jacob, Ashley, and Prince were the only people at the school. At least, he thought they were the only people at the school. How could the glass have broken all by itself? There were a bunch of vases up on a high shelf, and it looked like one of the vases had fallen down and shattered into a million tiny pieces on the floor. But somebody had to have knocked over one of the vases. Vases don't break by themselves, do they?

"Let's go check it out," suggested Agent Putty. "But stay by me, and be careful," he instructed. "We don't know what made that glass break. It might have been the Mystery Man. In fact, he could be here right now, but we just can't see him because he might be invisible."

Agent Putty flipped on the light switch, and then he and Dr. Gold slowly walked inside the room and went over to the broken glass to take a look. Jacob, Ashley, and Prince all followed close behind.

"Don't step on any of the glass," warned Dr. Gold. "It's very sharp and dangerous—it can cut through your shoes and could even cut your feet." Dr. Gold needed the help of The Super Secret Special Powers Club to solve all the mysteries, but the most important thing for him was to make sure that Jacob, Ashley, and Prince stayed safe and didn't get hurt.

Once everyone was inside the room, they were careful not to step on any of the glass. It was spread out all over the floor, and it looked extremely sharp.

"Look!" exclaimed Prince. He pointed at the window on the other side of the room. "Somebody left that window open. Maybe the wind came through the window and knocked over one of the glass vases on the top shelf."

"Hmmm," said Agent Putty. He thought about Prince's comment for a second and then replied, "The wind is one possible explanation, but there really isn't much wind outside right now. So, I don't think it was the wind. It had to be something else."

Dr. Gold nodded his head in agreement.

"Maybe the janitor knocked down the vase, and then he escaped out the window so that he wouldn't get blamed and get in trouble for breaking all the glass," suggested Ashley. "Maybe the janitor is the Mystery Man," she added.

"Not so fast, Ashley," replied Agent Putty. "You might be right, but we need more proof. We can't just accuse someone of being a bad person until we have more evidence."

Ashley nodded her head in understanding. She remembered from the robbery at her dad's bank last year that Agent Putty had to find evidence to catch her dad's boss, Mr. Wentworth, who stole the money. Evidence is the stuff that bad guys leave behind, which proves that they committed a crime.

Dr. Gold agreed, "Agent Putty is right. Remember, Miss Klanner accused Johnny and Marcus of a crime without any evidence. She told the police that they stole her diamonds, and then the police arrested the boys even though there wasn't enough proof that they did it. We don't want to be like Miss Klanner and accuse anybody of anything without evidence."

"Also," Prince added, "the janitor is a very nice guy. He cleans up all the messes at our school, and he always has a big smile on his face. Whenever someone loses something—like a jacket or sweatshirt—he always helps look around the entire school to find it. I don't think he's a bad guy, and I definitely don't think he's the Mystery Man."

Dr. Gold knew that he wouldn't be able to solve the mystery on his own. He declared, "I think it's time for our Super Secret Special Powers Club to help by using their special powers." He then turned to Ashley and said, "Ashley, tell us what you can see using your special power to see things that used to be there."

"Okay," replied Ashley, "I'll try." Ashley stared at the highest shelf with all the vases. She could see a shadowy figure with a cowboy hat reaching up to the back of the top ledge and grabbing some metal containers. The containers looked like the metal gas tanks that you would connect to an outside barbecue, or maybe even the type of metal canisters that people use when they go scuba diving underwater.

Ashley let everyone know what she was seeing with her special power. "There's some guy with a cowboy hat grabbing some metal containers on the very top shelf. I can see his elbow hitting one of the glass vases and knocking it off the shelf onto the floor. It looks like he's putting several of the metal containers into a big backpack. I also can see the shadowy figure doing something with that big basket in the corner of the room. And then I can see him opening the window and crawling through the window with his stuffed backpack."

"Well," said Dr. Gold, "it certainly sounds like you are seeing the Mystery Man, especially with the cowboy hat."

"I've never seen the janitor wear a cowboy hat, so it's probably not the janitor," suggested Prince.

Agent Putty walked over to the basket in the corner of the room. It was labeled batteries, and it was completely empty. Agent Putty stated, "Looks like the Mystery Man stole a bunch of batteries. Maybe he's using the batteries to power his special invisibility machine."

Dr. Gold stared up at the top shelf. He then grabbed a little step stool and climbed up so he could see the top better. After looking around the top shelf for a bit, he reached way out and grabbed a metal canister located at the very back. It was the only remaining metal container there.

Agent Putty looked closely at the writing on the side of the metal canister, which had two big letters on it—an upper case 'H' and a lower case 'e.' Agent

Putty asked Dr. Gold, "Why is the container labeled 'He?' What kind of container is it? What's inside?"

"It's helium," answered Dr. Gold. "The letters 'H' and 'e' make up the official chemical symbol for helium gas," he explained.

Agent Putty thought to himself for a second and then said, "I wonder why the Mystery Man wanted containers of helium gas."

Jacob was excited. He thought he knew the answer to why the Mystery Man stole the metal containers filled with helium. Jacob didn't say anything but raised his hand high in the air—just like his teacher, Miss Darling, taught him on his first day of kindergarten. He remembered the rule that he wasn't supposed to talk until he raised his hand and was called on.

"Yes, Jacob," said Agent Putty. "Do you have an idea about why the Mystery Man wanted helium containers?"

Jacob blurted out, "For balloons!" He thought he had figured out the entire mystery because he was so smart. Jacob remembered that helium gas is used to blow up balloons for birthday parties so that the balloons float in the air.

Dr. Gold chuckled a little, and then he said, "That's an excellent guess, Jacob. But I don't think the Mystery Man was interested in blowing up balloons for a birthday party." He then added, "However, I have another theory."

"What is it?" asked Prince.

"Well," started Dr. Gold, "the Mystery Man is working with electricity and wants to keep it a secret. And usually, electricity is invisible, silent, and odorless."

"What's A – Door – Less?" asked Jacob, mispronouncing the word.

Ashley corrected Jacob, "It's O – Door – Less with an 'O,' not A – Door – Less. Odorless means that there's no smell. Odor means smell, so odorless means there isn't any smell." Ashley wanted to prove to Jacob that he wasn't the only smart kid in the family. She was trying to show off to Jacob that she also was very intelligent because she read tons of books and worked so hard in school.

"That's absolutely right, Ashley," said Dr. Gold as he patted her on the shoulder for being so clever. He then explained, "If you add a gas like helium to electricity, then you will be able to see, hear, and even smell the electricity."

"That makes perfect sense!" exclaimed Agent Putty. He agreed that Dr. Gold had figured out part of the mystery since he was such a brilliant scientist. Agent Putty concluded, "The Mystery Man must be stealing the helium containers because he doesn't want anyone to use the helium gas to stop him from being invisible. If we use helium gas, then we will be able to see, hear, and smell the electricity, which means the Mystery Man won't be able to stay invisible and hide."

Dr. Gold then added, "I also wonder if the Mystery Man is using the helium gas to power his special light control machine. Not only does he not want anyone to discover his invisibility, but maybe he's also stealing the gas canisters so he can control all the lights."

Just then, Principal Crabtree drove into the school's parking lot. She parked her car in her reserved space right in front of the school next to where Dr. Gold's car and Agent Putty's car were parked. As she got out of the car, she saw that the door was open to the maintenance building. Principal Crabtree was extremely concerned because the entrance to the maintenance building was supposed to be closed and locked. So, she quickly jogged over to the maintenance building to see what was going on. Dr. Gold, Agent Putty, and the kids were all standing in the room by the broken glass.

"WHAT IN THE WORLD IS GOING ON HERE?" screamed Principal Crabtree. "School is closed. What are you doing here? Who broke all this glass?"

"Please calm down," replied Dr. Gold in a friendly tone. He could tell that Principal Crabtree was angry after seeing all the broken glass. "I promise you that we didn't break this glass and that we are only trying to solve a bunch of mysteries."

Agent Putty then pulled out his wallet that had a shiny gold badge on the front of it. "I'm Agent Putty with the FBI," he explained as he showed Principal Crabtree his official FBI badge. "We're here to help," he added.

Principal Crabtree calmed down as soon as she saw Agent Putty's badge. She understood that an FBI agent was sort of like a policeman and that Agent Putty was there to help her and the school.

Since she had just arrived at the school, Principal Crabtree had no idea why Agent Putty, Dr. Gold, and the kids were at the school. So, she asked Agent Putty, "Does this have something to do with the stolen batteries and helium canisters?"

Dr. Gold could not believe what Principal Crabtree had just said. How did she already know that the batteries and helium were missing? Principal Crabtree wasn't even there when they discovered the missing items in the storage room. So, he asked her, "How do you know about the batteries and helium?"

"I'm the principal," answered Principal Crabtree, "that's why." She explained, "I know everything that happens at my school—it's my job. On the first day of school, when all the electricity mysteriously was turned off, somebody stole all of our school's batteries and helium tanks. We finally got another new shipment just a few days ago."

"Wait a minute," said Agent Putty, "are you talking about what happened on the first day of school and not about what happened this morning?"

"Of course," replied Principal Crabtree. "I have no idea about what happened this morning. I only arrived at the school a few minutes ago. Did something happen today that I should know about, other than the broken glass in this room?"

Agent Putty didn't answer her question, but he asked Principal Crabtree another question, "Did you report the stolen batteries and helium on the first day of school to the police?"

"Yes, of course, I did," answered Principal Crabtree. "But the police said that it was most likely just a prank by some students who had terrible behavior. Since there were no fingerprints or other evidence, we had no way of figuring out who stole the batteries and helium. The police guessed that some misbehaving students must have wanted the batteries for their video games and that they probably wanted helium to blow up balloons for a party. Fortunately, one of our generous neighbors, Miss Klanner, offered to donate one thousand dollars to the school to help pay for new batteries and helium."

Dr. Gold smiled after listening to Principal Crabtree's explanation. He had just solved some of the mystery. He had figured out what happened on the first day of school, and he now knew what the Mystery Man was trying to do at the school.

"Why are you smiling, Dad?" asked Prince as he noticed the look on his dad's face.

"I think I figured out what's going on here," replied Dr. Gold. "The Mystery Man must have been the one to turn off all the lights on the first day of school in order to steal all the batteries and helium. He needed the batteries to power his light control machine, and he wanted all the helium to keep anyone from discovering his invisibility. The Mystery Man must have returned to the school today to steal more batteries and helium since the school just received a whole new shipment."

Dr. Gold thought to himself for a moment, and then he told Principal Crabtree, "We need to find Miss Klanner right away. Can you tell us how to find her?"

"Miss Klanner?" questioned Principal Crabtree. She had no idea why Dr. Gold would want to find Miss Klanner. What did Miss Klanner have to do with the Mystery Man? Principal Crabtree asked, "Why are you asking about Miss Klanner?"

"Well," explained Dr. Gold, "I don't think Miss Klanner really is a good person who was just trying to help."

"What do you mean?" replied Principal Crabtree. "She was very generous to donate one thousand dollars to our school."

Dr. Gold replied, "I think Miss Klanner is somehow involved with the stolen batteries and helium. I don't think she donated money to the school simply to be nice. I think she knew the Mystery Man stole the batteries and helium, and she wanted the school to buy even more batteries and helium so the Mystery Man could steal those too."

Agent Putty then added, "Miss Klanner must be helping the Mystery Man. That's why she donated money to the school to buy more batteries and helium. And the Mystery Man must have had something to do with the missing diamonds from Klanner Jewels."

"That can't be," responded Principal Crabtree. "Miss Klanner has lived in this community all her life. I know a lot of people don't like her because she is involved with the KKK, but I just can't believe she's a criminal."

"I'm sorry to tell you," said Dr. Gold, "but we think Miss Klanner may be involved in some criminal activities with the Mystery Man. But first, we need to gather more evidence to prove it."

Principal Crabtree didn't want the Mystery Man or Miss Klanner to do any more bad things, so she tried to help Agent Putty and Dr. Gold with their investigation. She offered, "Well, Miss Klanner probably isn't at her jewelry store, Klanner Jewels, right now because it's too early in the morning and it isn't open yet."

Principal Crabtree then pulled out a little black address book from her purse. "Maybe you could see if she's at her house," she suggested. Principal Crabtree flipped to the page in her little black book with Miss Klanner's address information and told Agent Putty and Dr. Gold, "Miss Klanner lives about a mile down the road from the school in the big white building on the corner of Main Street. She lives in the top floor penthouse, number 10K."

"Thank you," replied Agent Putty. "That's very helpful."

"Is there anything else I can do to assist?" asked Principal Crabtree.

"Well, it might be a good idea to clean up this mess of glass?" Agent Putty suggested. "We don't want anyone to get cut or hurt."

"I can certainly do that," agreed Principal Crabtree.

Dr. Gold then asked Principal Crabtree, "Would you mind if we also took this last remaining helium canister? It may help us with our detective work. And if we find all the missing batteries and other helium containers, then we will be able to return them back to the school."

"No problem," Principal Crabtree replied. "Good luck," she added.

Dr. Gold then said to the kids, "Hurry into Agent Putty's car. We better head to Miss Klanner's penthouse as quickly as possible. We need to find her to figure out what really happened with the diamonds at Klanner Jewels and to stop the Mystery Man before he does any more bad things."

Jacob, Ashley, and Prince all jumped into the back of Agent Putty's car. Dr. Gold put the helium canister in the trunk of Agent Putty's car, and then he got in the front passenger seat, right next to Agent Putty.

Agent Putty waved goodbye to Principal Crabtree as he started the engine, and then he quickly raced the car away from the school toward Miss Klanner's building.

CHAPTER 11

MISS KLANNER'S PENTHOUSE

It took less than five minutes for Agent Putty to drive from the school to the big white building where Miss Klanner lived. Agent Putty was a speedy driver. Even though his car didn't look like a race car, it felt like Agent Putty drove as fast as a race car driver.

Miss Klanner's building was once of the fanciest buildings in the neighborhood. It was bright white, with gigantic columns in the front—kind of like the White House where the president of the United States lives. There was an enormous green grass lawn in front of the building and a big stone walkway from the parking area through the grass that led to the front entrance.

As soon as Agent Putty parked the car, everyone quickly jumped out—they were in a rush. Agent Putty and Dr. Gold immediately started jogging across the grass to the front entrance of the building. They didn't even bother walking on the stone walkway since they were in too much of a hurry. Jacob, Ashley, and Prince had to run behind them just to keep up.

When they got to the front of the building, they were all breathing heavily from jogging across the grass lawn. Agent Putty held the front door open for everyone and then followed them into the building. Near the two large entrance doors were three elevators and a staircase that led to the upper floors.

As Dr. Gold tried to catch his breath, he said to Agent Putty, "I hope you don't think we're going to run up ten flights of stairs to Miss Klanner's penthouse. I think we have enough time to wait for the elevator."

Agent Putty laughed and replied, "It sounds like you're getting a little out of shape, buddy. When we were younger, you used to run up the stairs even faster than me."

"Well, I guess I need to start exercising more," admitted Dr. Gold. "But today, we should take the elevator and save our energy for solving all the mysteries."

"Fine with me," agreed Agent Putty. "You're the boss."

Jacob then pushed the up button for the elevator. He always loved to press elevator buttons—ever since he was a very young kid who could barely walk. Ashley also liked to push elevator buttons, but she let Jacob do it himself this time because she didn't want to argue with him. Ashley knew that every time she tried to press an elevator button, Jacob would throw a fit.

Luckily, the elevator arrived pretty quickly, and they didn't have to wait long at all. "What floor?" asked Jacob as soon as they got on the elevator.

"Tenth floor," answered Dr. Gold. "We're going to the penthouse on the top floor, number 10K."

Jacob pushed the button with a ten on it. It was a good thing that Jacob wasn't a little kid anymore. When he was a toddler, he liked to push all of the buttons inside the elevator, which meant you would have to wait and stop at every single floor. Jacob once got in a lot of trouble for doing that at a hotel while the Pea family was on vacation. Other hotel guests on the same elevator got very angry after Jacob pushed all the buttons. It felt like it took 20 minutes for the hotel elevator to stop at every single one of the floors before making it to the lobby at the bottom.

This time the elevator went straight up to the tenth floor without stopping. Agent Putty led everyone down the hall. And there, at the end of the hall, was a dark red door with 10K written in bright white paint on the front. It was the same bright white as the rest of the building.

Agent Putty knocked on the door and announced, "Miss Klanner, please open the door. This is Agent Putty with the FBI."

A very quiet voice came from inside the room, "Coming. I'll be there in just a second."

Agent Putty, Dr. Gold, and the kids waited patiently at the front door. After less than a minute, the door was unlocked and slowly opened.

There, in front of the open door, was Miss Klanner. She was a short, thin older woman who looked like she was about 70 years old. Miss Klanner wore a fancy, long dress, a necklace with pearls as big as marbles around her neck, ruby and sapphire bracelets on each wrist, and large, shiny diamond earrings hanging from her ears. She also had on several expensive-looking rings with different colored sparkly jewels. Miss Klanner had dyed platinum blonde hair, and her face was full of makeup with dark blue eyeshadow over her eyelids and bright red lipstick on her lips.

"What can I do for you, officer," asked Miss Klanner in a sweet and polite voice.

"Actually," replied Agent Putty in a serious manner, "I'm not a police officer. I'm an agent with the FBI, and I would like to ask you a few questions." Agent Putty then pulled out his wallet and showed Miss Klanner his gold FBI badge.

"Of course," responded Miss Klanner. "I would be happy to help if I can. I'm just an old lady who owns the local jewelry store, Klanner Jewels. I have no idea how I can assist you." Miss Klanner sounded very innocent. She asked Agent Putty, "What's this all about?"

"Would you mind telling us what happened with the stolen diamonds from your jewelry store?" asked Agent Putty.

Miss Klanner thought to herself for a little bit, and then she eventually answered, "I already explained everything to the police. That Asian boy and that Black boy stole all my diamonds. I saw them do it. They should be thrown in jail."

Agent Putty could tell that Miss Klanner was lying. He had lots of experience talking with criminals, and he could see by Miss Klanner's facial expressions and eye movements that she was hiding something. Agent Putty was using the training he received at a special FBI school to read Miss Klanner's face, so he knew that she wasn't telling the truth.

Dr. Gold also suspected that Miss Klanner was lying. He thought she was falsely accusing Johnny and Marcus of a crime just because she didn't like their skin color.

"I only have one more question," said Agent Putty. "Why did you decide to donate money to the local elementary school?"

Miss Klanner was silent for several seconds. She was thinking of an answer to Agent Putty's question but didn't immediately know what to say. Agent Putty could tell that she was guilty because an honest person telling the truth would have been able to answer such a simple question easily.

Finally, after what seemed like a long time, Miss Klanner responded, "Oh, yes, I completely forgot about my very generous donation to the school. I was only trying to be a good person, and I felt bad that someone took all the batteries and helium. That poor school—I donated the money just to be nice."

"Thank you, Miss Klanner," responded Agent Putty. "You've been very helpful, and those are all my questions."

After Agent Putty finished talking, Miss Klanner responded, "Well, I hope I was able to help you. Now I need to go hurry up and get ready to open up my jewelry store." As she closed the front door, she waved goodbye and said, "Have a nice day."

Dr. Gold, Jacob, Ashley, and Prince just stared at Agent Putty. They couldn't understand why he didn't ask Miss Klanner more questions. Agent Putty didn't even ask her anything about the Mystery Man.

"Why did you stop asking Miss Klanner questions?" Dr. Gold said to Agent Putty after Miss Klanner shut the door. "Why didn't you try to find out more information?"

"Because," answered Agent Putty, "Miss Klanner already told me everything that I need to know."

"What do you mean?" asked Ashley. She added, "Miss Klanner just said that Johnny and Marcus stole her diamonds and that she was only trying to be nice by donating money to the school to buy new batteries and helium. How did that help?" Ashley didn't think that Miss Klanner had told them anything useful.

Agent Putty responded, "It's not really *what* Miss Klanner said that was helpful. It's *how* she said it that was helpful. With my special FBI training, I could tell that she was totally lying and trying to hide something. Her eyes and facial expressions gave everything away."

"So, why didn't you arrest her?" asked Prince. He thought that if Miss Klanner was guilty of a crime, she should be arrested and sent to jail.

"That's a good question," replied Agent Putty. "But we still don't have enough evidence to prove that Miss Klanner committed a crime. We suspect that she's guilty, but we need to prove it first with evidence."

"And I know exactly where we can go to get the evidence," said Dr. Gold. He was smiling again, which is what he did whenever he solved a mystery. "I agree with Agent Putty that Miss Klanner is hiding something. And I believe the answer might be at her jewelry store, Klanner Jewels."

"I think you're right," responded Agent Putty. "But first, we need to visit Johnny and Marcus to hear their side of the story. So, that's where we're headed next."

CHAPTER 12

THE JUDGE AT THE COURTHOUSE

After visiting Miss Klanner, Agent Putty then drove Dr. Gold and the kids to the courthouse. It was a long drive on the freeway since the courthouse was located far away in the big city.

Dr. Gold called Mrs. Pea from his cell phone while Agent Putty was driving. After a few rings, she answered the phone, and then Dr. Gold said, "Hello, Mrs. Pea. This is Dr. Gold."

"Oh, hi," replied Mrs. Pea. "What can I do for you? I'm about to go to court to help Johnny and Marcus."

"That's actually why I'm calling," responded Dr. Gold. "I'm with Agent Putty and the kids right now. We just finished talking to Miss Klanner, and now we need to talk to Johnny and Marcus to hear their side of the story."

"Okay," said Mrs. Pea. "That shouldn't be a problem at all. I think Miss Klanner has been lying about the stolen diamonds from her jewelry store. I already heard Johnny and Marcus tell their story, and I believe that they are completely innocent. We're about to go in front of a judge a little bit later, and I'm going to tell the judge that Miss Klanner wasn't telling the truth and that the boys should be allowed to go home to their families."

"Great," replied Dr. Gold. "We'll be there as soon as we can. See you soon."

"All right, bye," responded Mrs. Pea as they both hung up their phones.

Agent Putty, Dr. Gold, and the kids arrived in the big city about 20 minutes later. After Agent Putty parked the car in the large parking structure next to the courthouse, they all walked over to meet Mrs. Pea, who was waiting for them outside the building.

"Hello, everyone. Good to see you all," said Mrs. Pea.

Ashley and Jacob both said, "Hi, Mom!" Agent Putty, Dr. Gold, and Prince also all said hello to Mrs. Pea.

"Why don't you follow me inside the courthouse?" suggested Mrs. Pea. "Johnny and Marcus are waiting for us in a special room right now. We can go talk to them before we need to go in front of the judge."

Mrs. Pea led Agent Putty, Dr. Gold, and the kids up the giant marble staircase at the courthouse and down a long hallway to a room that two policemen were guarding.

"I'm here to see my clients," said Mrs. Pea to the policemen.

"Yes, ma'am," replied one of the policemen. The other policeman then opened the door for everyone. The police officers recognized Mrs. Pea and knew that she was the lawyer for Johnny and Marcus.

Inside the room, Johnny and Marcus were both sitting at a large wooden table wearing suits and ties. Mrs. Pea had told them that it was important for them to dress up as nicely as possible for the judge since going in front of the judge in a courtroom is a very serious occasion.

"Hello, boys," said Agent Putty as he walked into the room. "I'm Agent Putty with the FBI, and I'm here to ask you a few questions." He then pulled out his wallet and showed them his shiny gold FBI badge.

Johnny and Marcus both looked over to Mrs. Pea for permission to talk to Agent Putty. They weren't sure if they could trust Agent Putty, so they wanted to check with Mrs. Pea first since she was their attorney—and it was her job to protect them.

"It's okay, boys," Mrs. Pea informed Johnny and Marcus. "Agent Putty is on our side, and he's trying to help. Please go ahead and answer his questions."

"Okay," responded both Johnny and Marcus at the same time.

Agent Putty then asked, "Did you steal the diamonds from Klanner Jewels?"

"No way!" immediately exclaimed Johnny. "We'd never do anything like that."

"Yeah," added Marcus. "We didn't do anything wrong. We were just playing basketball, and then all of a sudden, the police arrested us and told us that we were in trouble for stealing diamonds."

Agent Putty believed the boys. Using his FBI training, he could tell by their eyes and facial expressions that they were telling the whole truth.

"Now, I need you to think back a few days," said Agent Putty to the boys. "Did you ever hang around Klanner Jewels?"

Johnny and Marcus looked at each other, and then Johnny answered, "Yes, we kind of did. We actually walked by Klanner Jewels on the way to the basketball courts at the park to play basketball. There was a big shiny basketball made of gold in the display window of the jewelry store."

Marcus then continued, "But all we did was stop and look at the gold basketball through the window. We thought it looked so cool. I swear we didn't steal anything. Right after stopping outside the jewelry store, we walked straight to the park to play basketball. We never even went inside the jewelry store."

"Don' worry, I believe you," replied Agent Putty in a calm voice. "Is there anything else that you saw by the jewelry store that looked strange or out of place? Anything at all that you remember?"

Johnny and Marcus thought to themselves for a minute.

Marcus then said, "Hey, Johnny, remember that weird-looking guy with the big hat that went into the jewelry store?"

"Oh yeah," replied Johnny. "There was a strange guy with a big black cowboy hat who went into the store. He was wearing a dark black coat, black jeans, and black boots, and he had on dark sunglasses. I definitely remember that guy because he never took off his sunglasses—even in the store. We could see him through the front window."

Agent Putty, Dr. Gold, and the kids knew exactly who Johnny and Marcus were talking about. The two boys had just identified the Mystery Man. But what was the Mystery Man doing at Klanner Jewels?

"Thank you," said Agent Putty to the boys, "that was extremely helpful." "Don't worry," he added, "Mrs. Pea is a great lawyer, and she's going to help you with the judge. Meanwhile, I think it's time for me to go visit Klanner Jewels with Dr. Gold and the kids to figure out the mystery of who actually stole the diamonds."

"I wish you all the best of luck," said Mrs. Pea. "The only thing we know for sure is that it wasn't Johnny and Marcus who stole the diamonds.

After everyone said their goodbyes, Agent Putty left the courthouse with Dr. Gold and the children.

Mrs. Pea then walked with Johnny and Marcus down the hallway to the courtroom to see the judge. The two police officers who had been guarding their room followed Mrs. Pea and the two boys into the courtroom.

Johnny and Marcus's parents were already seated at the back of the courtroom when Mrs. Pea and the boys got there. They waved to Johnny and Marcus, but Mrs. Pea and the two boys weren't allowed to talk to them. Instead, they had to go directly to a table near the judge's large desk at the front of the room.

Everyone sat and waited silently for a few minutes in the courtroom. Eventually, the judge entered from a separate door at the side of the room. The judge was a very large man with a shaved head and a dark black beard. He was wearing a long black robe, and he had an extremely serious expression on his face.

As the judge walked slowly up to his big desk at the very front of the courtroom, a man standing next to the desk—who looked like a police officer—announced to everyone, "I'm Officer Watson, the bailiff for this courtroom. All rise and come to order. The Superior Court is now in session with the Honorable Judge Jenkins presiding."

Everyone in the courtroom followed the bailiff's instructions and stood up from their seats. As they were standing, Mrs. Pea leaned over and quickly explained to Johnny and Marcus that the bailiff is kind of like a special police officer who helps the judge manage the courtroom.

As soon as the judge went to sit down, the bailiff directed everyone, "You may now be seated." While everyone in the courtroom sat back down, the bailiff then handed Judge Jenkins some papers and informed him, "Your honor, this is case number 42 dash 0617892, People versus Johnny Chang and Marcus Smith."

Judge Jenkins looked directly at Johnny and Marcus and said, "Please raise your right hand."

Johnny and Marcus did exactly what the judge told them to do and raised their right hands in the air.

Judge Jenkins then asked, "Do you promise to tell the truth, the whole truth, and nothing but the truth, so help you, God?"

Johnny and Marcus each responded, "Yes, I do."

"Okay," said Judge Jenkins, "then, why don't we get started?"

Mrs. Pea then stood up from her seat and said, "Your honor, there has been an enormous miscarriage of justice in this case."

Johnny and Marcus didn't know that a 'miscarriage of justice' meant an enormous mistake, but they knew that Mrs. Pea was one of the best lawyers in town and that she was going to help them with all of her legal knowledge.

"Please explain," responded Judge Jenkins. He folded his hands on his desk, leaned forward in his chair, and he looked like he was going to listen very closely to what Mrs. Pea had to say.

"My clients, Johnny Chang and Marcus Smith, never stole any diamonds," continued Mrs. Pea. "They simply walked by Klanner Jewels on the way to play basketball at the park. They've never even been inside Klanner Jewels. The police checked Klanner Jewels for fingerprints, and there weren't any fingerprints from Johnny or Marcus inside Klanner Jewels. When the police arrested Johnny and Marcus at the park, they didn't have any diamonds on them. The police also did a full and complete search of Johnny and Marcus's homes, and the police didn't find any diamonds there either.

Accordingly, the police should never have been allowed to arrest Johnny and Marcus without more evidence. The only proof that the police had is that Miss Klanner said she saw Johnny and Marcus steal her diamonds. We believe that Miss Klanner—a member of the KKK—lied to the police because she doesn't like Johnny or Marcus or anyone else who doesn't have white skin. Therefore, pursuant to state law, the Sixth Amendment to the United States Constitution, and the 1972 Supreme Court case of Barker versus Wingo, Johnny and Marcus should be found innocent of all charges and allowed to go home to their families."

Judge Jenkins looked intensely at Mrs. Pea for a minute, and then he looked over and stared at Johnny and Marcus. Without saying a word, Judge Jenkins uncrossed his folded hands, grabbed a pen, and then slowly tapped the pen on his enormous wooden desk in the front of the courtroom. After a couple of minutes of thinking while the room remained silent, Judge Jenkins finally spoke in a deep serious voice, "Johnny Chang and Marcus Smith, did you steal the diamonds?"

Johnny and Marcus both quickly and clearly answered, "No, your honor."

"In that case," said Judge Jenkins as he banged a small wooden hammer—called a gavel—that he had on his desk, "I find you not guilty, and you are free to go. Your attorney, Mrs. Pea, is completely correct. There is not sufficient evidence to convict you of a crime, and all charges against you are hereby dropped."

Mrs. Pea took a deep breath and then smiled at Johnny and Marcus. She explained to them with excitement, "It's done! We did it! You're free to go!"

Johnny and Marcus both had an enormous sigh of relief and then hugged Mrs. Pea. They also thanked her for all of her help.

Johnny and Marcus's parents quickly walked up to the front of the courtroom to hug their sons and thank Mrs. Pea for saving them from jail. All the parents were crying tears of happiness.

As they were celebrating the victory, Johnny asked Mrs. Pea, "But what about Miss Klanner? What actually happened to the diamonds at Klanner Jewels?"

"That's not our problem," responded Mrs. Pea. "But, don't worry, Agent Putty and Dr. Gold are going to try to solve that mystery." Mrs. Pea didn't know that Jacob, Ashley, and Prince had special powers and that they also were going to help Agent Putty and Dr. Gold solve the mystery by using their special powers as detectives.

CHAPTER 13

KLANNER JEWELS

While Mrs. Pea was with Johnny and Marcus at the courthouse, Agent Putty, Dr. Gold, Jacob, Ashley, and Prince arrived at Klanner Jewels. They arrived in record time since Agent Putty drove so fast. He had even turned on the siren and flashing lights on his FBI car to get to the jewelry store as quickly as possible.

Before they all entered Klanner Jewels, Dr. Gold said, "Wait, I think we need Ashley's help first."

Ashley knew that Dr. Gold wanted her to use her special power to see things that used to be there but weren't there anymore. "Okay," she said, "no problem."

Ashley looked outside the jewelry store at the front door and front window. It was hard for her to tell which shadowy figures were important because so many people had walked by the front of the store. Then she finally focused on two specific shadowy figures that walked to the front of the store.

"What do you see?" Dr. Gold asked Ashley.

"I think I see Johnny and Marcus," Ashley answered.

"How can you be sure?" asked Agent Putty.

"Well," replied Ashley, "I see two shadowy figures walking down the street, and one of them looks like he is bouncing a shadowy basketball. The two figures stop at the front window for a little bit, and then they keep walking down the street."

"That definitely sounds like Johnny and Marcus based on the story they told us at the courthouse," said Prince.

Jacob looked at the front window of Klanner Jewels and pointed excitedly. "Look, everyone!" he exclaimed. "It's the gold basketball that Johnny and Marcus talked about."

Jacob was right. A shiny basketball that looked like it was made out of solid gold was sitting on a glass pedestal in the front window of the jewelry store.

"Why would someone steal the diamonds and not also steal that gold basketball?" asked Prince. He thought the gold basketball must have been worth a fortune and that a robber would want to steal that fancy basketball first.

Agent Putty answered Prince's question, "Believe it or not, diamonds actually are worth a lot more money than gold. Also, diamonds are a lot smaller and lighter than gold, so they are easier for criminals to steal and hide. That gold basketball must weigh a ton, so it would be much harder to steal."

Dr. Gold then suggested, "Why don't we go into the store now and let Ashley tell us what else she can see with her special power?"

Agent Putty and Dr. Gold led the way into the store, and Jacob, Ashley, and Prince followed them. There was a nicely dressed woman working at the front of the store, but Miss Klanner wasn't there. After everyone walked into the store, the woman introduced herself in a friendly voice, "Hi, everyone, my name is Ruby—like the beautiful gem. Please let me know if I can be of any assistance."

"Thank you, Ruby," replied Agent Putty. He then said in a serious manner, "My name is Agent Putty with the FBI. We're here to investigate the mystery of the stolen diamonds." Agent Putty pulled out his wallet and showed Ruby his gold FBI badge.

"Yes, sir," responded Ruby. "But I thought Miss Klanner said that those two boys stole all the diamonds."

"Well," said Agent Putty, "that's what we're here to find out."

Ashley looked all around the jewelry store. It was a small store with fancy and expensive-looking jewelry all around. There were rings, bracelets, earrings, necklaces, and watches—and they were all very shiny and sparkly.

"Can you see the Mystery Man?" Dr. Gold asked Ashley.

Ashley used her special power to look as hard as she could at all the shadowy figures that used to be in the store, and then she finally spotted the Mystery Man wearing the cowboy hat. Unlike some of the other shadowy figures that she saw, the figure that looked like the Mystery Man was very clear. Ashley could tell that he had been in the jewelry store recently because his shadowy figure almost looked like a real person. When she used her extraordinary power, things that used to be there a long time ago appeared fuzzy to her, but something that was there only a short time ago looked clear.

"I can see the shadowy figure of the Mystery Man," replied Ashley. "He is walking to the cash register at the front of the store. It looks like he is talking to some woman. Then they both go through the door at the back of the store together. They both sort of disappear after that." Ashley was confused and disappointed. She couldn't understand where the two shadowy figures went and how they just vanished. She wanted to help Agent Putty and Dr. Gold, but her special power didn't seem to be working.

"That's strange," mumbled Agent Putty. "How could they both just disappear? I wonder why Ashley isn't able to see them using her special power."

Dr. Gold thought for a moment, and then he said, "Maybe Jacob could help." He looked at Jacob and nicely asked, "Jacob, do you think you might be able to use your special power?"

Jacob was extremely excited and felt like a superhero. He was finally going to do some real detective work with his unique power as part of The Super Secret Special Powers Club.

"Yeah," replied Jacob, "I'm ready." Jacob stood very still, and he tried to see through other peoples' eyes. He was silent for a minute, and then he got a big grin on his face. "I think I see Miss Klanner and the Mystery Man," he declared.

"Are you sure?" asked Agent Putty.

"Yeah, I'm pretty sure," responded Jacob. "But it's really weird."

"What do you mean?" asked Dr. Gold.

"Well," said Jacob, "I can see Miss Klanner looking at the Mystery Man, and I can see the Mystery Man looking at Miss Klanner. They are in some sort of dark room, and they are surrounded by shelves filled with food. There is a big door in front of them, which looks like it is made of metal. Miss Klanner is shivering, but the Mystery Man looks like he is okay because he has on a warm coat."

"That doesn't make any sense," responded Ashley. She didn't understand what Jacob could be seeing. What kind of room is dark with food in it? And why would Miss Klanner be shivering? Even though it was winter, it wasn't actually that cold outside.

Dr. Gold thought to himself for a minute, and then he turned to ask Ruby a question. "Excuse me, Ruby," he said.

Ruby was busy polishing some jewelry in one of the cases, but she looked up when she heard Dr. Gold's voice. "Yes, I am here to help," she replied.

Dr. Gold then asked Ruby, "Do you happen to know what this store used to be before Miss Klanner bought it and turned it into Klanner Jewels?"

"Of course," responded Ruby. "I've lived in this neighborhood my whole life. When I was younger, this used to be a small restaurant that sold deli sandwiches. It used to be called Cannelli's Deli."

"That's it!" exclaimed Dr. Gold. "I think I know what's going on here."

"What is it?" asked Agent Putty. He knew that Dr. Gold had figured out a mystery, but he still didn't know what the answer was.

Dr. Gold didn't answer the question right away, but he simply said to Agent Putty, "Let's go get the canister of helium out of your car that we borrowed from the school. I think we're going to need it."

Agent Putty knew how smart Dr. Gold was, and he knew that it would be best to follow his directions. So, Agent Putty and Dr. Gold walked back to the trunk of Agent Putty's car to get the helium container with the kids.

Once they were outside by the car, Dr. Gold explained, "I think Miss Klanner and the Mystery Man are hiding in the refrigerator."

"What refrigerator?" asked Agent Putty. "Why would a jewelry store have a refrigerator?" Agent Putty was still confused. He didn't understand what Dr. Gold was talking about.

"It must be a hidden refrigerator," responded Dr. Gold. "Back when the store used to be a sandwich shop, I bet you there was a large refrigerator in the back room. When Miss Klanner turned this place into a jewelry store, she probably left the refrigerator there since it would be too much trouble to remove."

"That makes perfect sense," said Agent Putty. He finally understood what Dr. Gold had already figured out. That must have been what Jacob saw with his special power—Miss Klanner and the Mystery Man were in a cold, dark room with food on the shelves and a metal door. The two of them must be hiding in the large, old refrigerator.

Dr. Gold added, "We're going to need to use the helium to see and catch the Mystery Man, or else he might use his machine to turn invisible."

"Let's do it," agreed Agent Putty. "I'm ready."

Agent Putty, Dr. Gold, and the kids then went back into the jewelry store.

Agent Putty said to Ruby, “We’re going to take a quick peek in the back room—if that’s okay with you.”

“Please, be my guest,” responded Ruby. “If you need anything else, just give me a holler.”

Agent Putty opened the door to the back room and turned on all the lights. There was almost nothing there. It looked like it was a fairly empty, windowless storage room. A broom was in one corner, and a small table was pushed up against the back wall. There were some cardboard boxes on one side wall, and the other side wall was completely blank.

“There’s no refrigerator here,” observed Prince.

“Yeah,” agreed Ashley, “it’s just an empty room.”

“Try using your special power again,” Dr. Gold suggested to Ashley.

Ashley looked around the room. She saw the shadowy figures of the Mystery Man and Miss Klanner, but they seemed to disappear by the completely blank side wall.

"I can't understand it," Ashley said. "I see the two shadowy figures, but they just disappear by that empty side wall." Ashley was so confused. How did the shadowy figures both disappear? Where could they have gone?

Dr. Gold walked slowly up to the side wall and gently rubbed his open hand along the edge. "There must be a way in," he said to himself.

Agent Putty knew he could help, especially since he had a lot of FBI training on finding criminals in their hiding places. After looking closely at the walls and everything else in the room, Agent Putty finally said, "Aha!" He pointed to a little button on the other side of the room, which was partly hidden behind the cardboard boxes.

"Wait," said Dr. Gold before Agent Putty could push the button. "Let's get ready to turn on the helium, just in case the Mystery Man tries to escape using his invisibility machine."

Agent Putty nodded his head in agreement. "How about I count to three, and then we go on three? I'll press the button, and you stay ready to turn on the helium."

Dr. Gold replied, "That works for me." He then added, "Kids, you better wait over in the corner by the mop so that you don't get hurt. Agent Putty is here to protect us, and I don't want you to get in the way."

Jacob, Ashley, and Prince all said okay, and they went to the corner of the room as Dr. Gold had instructed.

"All right, let's do this," said Agent Putty. He counted, "One. Two. Three." And then he pressed the button on the wall.

At first, nothing happened. But then, after several seconds of delay, the blank wall started to slowly rise up into the ceiling, kind of like a garage door. Behind the first wall was another wall with a big metal door in the center—it was the door to a giant refrigerator. The old refrigerator from the deli was hiding behind the wall the entire time.

Agent Putty grabbed the gun out of his jacket holster just in case, and then he used his other hand to open the refrigerator door. There, sitting and shivering in the refrigerator, was Miss Klanner. But the Mystery Man wasn't there.

Dr. Gold was ready, though. He turned on the helium canister using the metal knob at the top, and it made a hissing sound while releasing the helium gas. As the gas quickly floated into the refrigerator, there were flashes and sparks like lightning, a crackling sound like popcorn popping in the microwave, and a slight smell of smoke like after you blow out a candle. All of a sudden, the Mystery Man appeared out of nowhere. He had been sitting right next to Miss Klanner the whole time. The helium gas made it so that his invisibility machine no longer worked.

Agent Putty then said with a very high squeaky voice, "Please exit the refrigerator." He kind of sounded like a chipmunk because he had breathed in a bunch of the helium gas. Sometimes if you breathe helium gas, it makes your voice sound really high. Jacob, Ashley, and Prince started laughing a little at Agent Putty because he sounded so funny.

Agent Putty waited a bit for the gas to go away, and then he tried to talk again with a much more official-sounding voice. "I am Agent Putty with the FBI. Please exit the refrigerator," he instructed Miss Klanner and the Mystery Man. He then added with a very serious voice, "You have the right to remain silent. Anything you say can and will be used against you in a court of law. You have the right to speak to an attorney, and to have an attorney present during any questioning. If you cannot afford a lawyer, one will be provided for you at government expense."

As Miss Klanner and the Mystery Man slowly walked out of the refrigerator, Miss Klanner started to cry.

"It was all his idea," Miss Klanner cried out with a sobbing voice. "He has the diamonds. They are all in a bag in his jacket. He told me that if I paid him with diamonds, he would help me get rid of Black, Asian, Hispanic, and Jewish people. Those boys didn't steal the diamonds. I only told the police that they stole the diamonds so that they would have to go to jail."

The Mystery Man didn't say a word. He just stood there silently with his face covered by a big cowboy hat and dark sunglasses.

Dr. Gold looked into the refrigerator as Miss Klanner and the Mystery Man were leaving. A bunch of the stolen batteries and helium canisters from the school were in the very back of the giant refrigerator. He knew that Principal Crabtree would be thrilled to have all those items returned to the school.

"I think we also found the missing school supplies," Dr. Gold announced.

Miss Klanner was whimpering like a sad puppy dog. "He told me to help him steal those batteries and helium containers," whined Miss Klanner. "He said that he needed those school supplies to get rid of everyone who wasn't white and Christian. That's why I paid him the diamonds and helped him steal all those supplies from the school. He promised that he would help me get all those Black, Brown, and Jewish people out of this country."

The Mystery Man still didn't say anything. He was as quiet as a mouse.

Agent Putty then handed Dr. Gold two pairs of handcuffs that he had been storing inside his jacket. "Why don't you go ahead and put these on our criminals' wrists?" he said to Dr. Gold.

Dr. Gold grabbed the handcuffs from Agent Putty while Miss Klanner cried uncontrollably. The Mystery Man continued to stand there silently, but then an evil-looking grin started to form on his face. It looked like he was up to something, even though he was just standing there like a statue.

As soon as Dr. Gold reached to put the handcuffs on the Mystery Man's wrists, the Mystery Man jumped headfirst into the cardboard boxes along the side of the room. All of the lights in the storage room suddenly turned off.

The Mystery Man had hidden his light control machine behind the cardboard boxes. When he dove at the boxes, he was able to hit the switch on the light control machine before anyone could stop him.

Even though Agent Putty had a gun, he wasn't going to use it in a dark room to stop the Mystery Man, or else he might risk shooting the wrong person.

Prince would have used his special power to stop the Mystery Man by moving extremely fast while everything else slowed down, but he couldn't do it in the dark. He wasn't able to see anything in the blackness while all the lights were off, and he didn't want to risk hurting himself or his friends by running into them.

Before anyone else could do anything, the Mystery Man quickly snuck out of the storage room while carrying the light control machine, and then he ran out the front door of the jewelry store. He moved so fast in the dark that nobody was able to stop him. Somehow, the Mystery Man could see perfectly, even though he wore dark sunglasses in the pitch-black storage room. Everyone else was completely blind since there were no lights and no windows to allow in any sunlight.

Less than a minute later, all the lights in the storage room came back on. The Mystery Man had escaped. Meanwhile, Agent Putty, Dr. Gold, Jacob,

Ashley, and Prince could not believe what had happened. Miss Klanner was just standing there crying.

Agent Putty ran out the door to see if he could catch the Mystery Man, but it was too late. He was gone. The Mystery Man was nowhere to be found.

Dr. Gold put the handcuffs on Miss Klanner's wrists as Agent Putty walked back into the storage room.

"Did you find him?" asked Dr. Gold.

"Nope," answered Agent Putty disappointedly. "It looks like the Mystery Man has escaped. He might have gotten away this time, but we are never going to stop looking for him."

"But he has all my diamonds," cried Miss Klanner. "What about my diamonds?"

"Well," answered Agent Putty, "I don't think you're going to need those diamonds where you're going. You helped the Mystery Man steal supplies from the school, and you falsely accused two innocent boys of stealing from your jewelry store. The only place you're going is to jail, and you're going to be there for a very long time."

Agent Putty then said to Dr. Gold, "Is it okay with you if I drive Miss Klanner straight to the police station?"

"No problem," answered Dr. Gold. "I can call Mr. and Mrs. Pea, and I'm sure they can come pick us up and drive the rest of us home."

"Okay, sounds like a plan," replied Agent Putty. "Talk to you soon," he said as he walked Miss Klanner in handcuffs out the front door of the jewelry store toward his black FBI car.

CHAPTER 14

WOMAN AT THE JEWELRY STORE

After Agent Putty left the jewelry store, Dr. Gold glanced at Jacob, Ashley, and Prince. The kids looked very sad and disappointed that the Mystery Man had gotten away.

"You kids did great," said Dr. Gold with a cheery voice. He was very proud of how much they helped with the investigation and all the detective work.

"But we failed," responded Prince sadly. Prince knew that the Mystery Man had escaped, so he didn't understand why his dad said they did a good job.

"No, we didn't completely fail," replied Dr. Gold. "We caught Miss Klanner, and we collected enough evidence to prove that she is a bad criminal. Thanks to our detective work, she'll now be punished and go to jail. The Mystery Man may have gotten away this time, but we were extremely close to catching him. Don't worry; we'll get him next time."

Prince felt better after his dad's explanation. Dr. Gold was right—they did do a good job. Miss Klanner was a bad criminal, and now she would need to go to jail for breaking the law. Miss Klanner would never have been caught if it wasn't for the help of The Super Secret Special Powers Club.

"Was I a good helper?" asked Jacob. He had tried his best to do a good job, but he wasn't sure if he succeeded.

"Of course," replied Dr. Gold. "We couldn't have solved the mystery without you. You and your special power helped save the day."

After hearing Dr. Gold's praise, Jacob had a beaming smile on his face. He was so happy that he was able to help.

Ashley then added, "I guess our Super Secret Special Powers Club still has some more work to do. We have to stop the Mystery Man from doing any more bad things."

"You're right," responded Dr. Gold. "But not today. We've already done more than enough good work for one day. We'll have to save catching the Mystery Man for another day."

Dr. Gold then put his arm around his son Prince. "Come on, son," he said, "why don't we go outside and call Mr. and Mrs. Pea to see if they'll give us all a ride home?" He then said to Ashley and Jacob, "You two can stay here inside the store if you want and look at all the pretty jewelry until your parents come to pick us up."

"Okay," replied Ashley and Jacob.

After Dr. Gold and Prince walked out the front door of the jewelry store, Jacob tapped Ashley on the shoulder.

"What is it?" asked Ashley.

"Look," replied Jacob as he pointed across the room.

At the other end of the jewelry store, by the fancy watches, was a woman who looked exactly like Mrs. Gold. It had to be Mrs. Gold. She looked just like the woman in the picture that Dr. Gold and Prince had at their house.

When the woman saw that Ashley and Jacob were staring at her, she put her index finger up to her mouth—which is the symbol to be quiet. She wrote something down on a piece of paper, left the note on the jewelry counter, and then she suddenly disappeared.

Ashley and Jacob were shocked. This was just like what had happened after the robbery at their father's bank last year—the woman who looked like Mrs. Gold appeared and then quickly vanished.

Ashley walked up to the counter, grabbed the piece of paper, and then read what it said out loud to Jacob, "I am undercover. Don't tell anyone except for Dr. Gold and Prince."

"Why would Prince's mom say that she is under the covers?" asked Jacob, who was a bit confused. "Does that mean she's in her bed?"

Ashley laughed a little at Jacob's question. "No, silly," she responded. "Mrs. Gold didn't say that she was under the covers. She said that she was undercover." Ashley explained, "Undercover means that you are pretending to be a bad guy when you really are a good guy. It's a way to trick the bad guys so it will be easier to catch them. Bad guys like to hide from the good guys. But, if the bad guys think that you also are a bad guy, then they won't hide from you."

"I think I get it," said Jacob. "Maybe Prince's mom can help us catch the Mystery Man. She can pretend to be a bad criminal just like the Mystery

Man, and then she can trick him so that we can catch him and take him to jail."

Ashley was impressed with Jacob. She told him, "That actually sounds like an excellent plan. It would be the perfect trap for the Mystery Man."

All of a sudden, the note just disappeared right out of Ashley's hand.

"How did the paper do that?" asked Jacob. One second it was in Ashley's hand, and the next second it was gone.

"I have no idea," responded Ashley. "I was holding the note, and then it just vanished." Ashley checked all around her, just to make sure that she didn't drop the paper. How could the message have just disappeared out of her hand?

"We need to find Prince's mom," said Jacob. "We have to tell Dr. Gold and Prince about her and the note," he added.

"Okay," replied Ashley, "but first, you need to calm down a little." She could tell that Jacob was getting a little too excited about seeing Mrs. Gold. "Let's go outside and talk to Dr. Gold and Prince."

Ashley and Jacob walked out of the jewelry store and saw Dr. Gold and Prince waiting outside the store. Ashley told them about what just happened with Mrs. Gold and the message.

"Are you sure she's gone?" asked Prince. He was very sad and upset that he didn't have a chance to see his mom. "Why didn't she stay to say hi to me and my dad?"

Dr. Gold responded, "I'm sure she has a good reason, son. Your mom loves you very much, but maybe it isn't safe for her to see us right now. If she's undercover and pretending to be a bad guy, then we have to keep her secret and not tell anyone else. We don't want the bad guys to find out since they might hurt her."

"Then, what can we do?" questioned Prince.

"Right now," answered Dr. Gold, "all we can do is wait. When the time is right, I'm sure your mom will give us a clue and let us know more about what's going on. For now, I think we've all earned a break. We already had a huge adventure today, and we can save the Mystery Man and Mrs. Gold for another day."

A minivan then pulled up right in front of the jewelry store. Mr. Pea was driving, and Mrs. Pea was in the front passenger seat. Mrs. Pea put down her window and said, "We're here! Are you ready to head home?"

Jacob got excited and whispered to Prince and Ashley, “Mom and Dad got us donuts.” He had used his special power to see using other people’s eyes, and he knew that there was a big box of fresh donuts waiting for them in the back seat.

Prince and Ashley couldn’t wait—they loved donuts. Even though they weren’t able to catch the Mystery Man, they were happy that Miss Klanner was going to jail—and they were ready to celebrate with some delicious donuts.

Dr. Gold opened the side door to the minivan, and the kids all climbed in first. Jacob went straight to the box of donuts, grabbed his favorite twisted, glazed kind, and then handed the rest of the box to Prince and Ashley.

As Dr. Gold went to get in the minivan, he turned and looked down the street. He thought he might have seen Mrs. Gold waving to him on the corner, but then she quickly disappeared. Dr. Gold deeply loved and missed his wife, but at least now, he was extremely happy to know that she really was alive and that he would get to see her again in the future.

ABOUT THE AUTHOR

Justin T. Miller wrote the first book in his Adventures of Prince and Ashley series, *The Super Secret Special Powers Club*, while his children were in elementary school. Miller understood what made his children excited to read and used these experiences to create a compelling story about two adventurous young detectives. Inspired by the positive responses from all the fantastic kids who read his first book and the complimentary reviews posted by their parents, he completed his second book, *The Mysterious Mystery Man*, in 2021.

Miller received a bachelor's degree from the University of California, Berkeley, and a law degree and master's degree in taxation from New York University School of Law. He is a nationally known tax and estate planning attorney, speaker, professor, and published author.

Miller lives with his wife, two children, and two dogs in Walnut Creek, California.

www.ingramcontent.com/pod-product-compliance
Lightning Source LLC
LaVergne TN
LVHW050632100826
845148LV00011B/1848

* 9 7 8 0 5 7 8 9 4 1 6 2 2 *